BOOK 3 OF THE FALL TRILOGY

We All Fall

This book is a work of fiction. Names, characters, places, and incidents are the product of the author's imagination or are used fictitiously. Any resemblance to actual events, locales, or persons, living or dead, is strictly coincidental.

WE ALL FALL © 2024 ARDEN COUTTS

Paperback ISBN: 979-8-9886620-9-9
eBook ISBN: 979-8-9886620-8-2

Published by CEI Media
Durham, NC
Printed in the United States of America
First Edition – November 2024

Editing by Hannah
G. Scheffer-Wentz, English Proper Editing Services & Novel Creature Books

Cover art by @artchameleon
Cover design & Interior layout by: Jbookdesigns

A note to readers:

It is strongly recommended that Book 1: _Fall Into Midnight_ and Book 2: _Fall Into Me_ should be read first. _We All Fall_ continues the plot in the trilogy's first and second books.

We are not broken. We are healing.

Scan the QR code below to enjoy the
playlist inspired by the book!

CHAPTER 1

James

Shawn reaches his hand out towards me, as if to help me up. Looking past his hand, all I see is his bloody, sooty face. I focus on his lips that are moving, but no sound is coming out. Finally, my brain registers what Shawn is saying:

"Get. Up."

I gasp awake and my world slowly comes into focus as the ringing in my ears grows louder. I can't seem to draw a breath, and my arm doesn't seem to move even though I'm telling it to. I try to roll off my back, but a sharp stabbing pain in my side stops me. I gasp for air and stare up at the cloudy sky. No, not cloudy—*smokey*.

I try to lift my head, and it seems to weigh more than it should. Looking down at my body, taking account of my injuries, my head begins to clear a bit. My arm is completely fucked. I can see the bone sticking out of the flesh of my forearm, but I can't feel anything.

I try to roll to my side again and manage to get my good arm under me so that I can prop myself up. Getting my knees under me, the rubble cuts into them. Leaning back, my knees take my weight. A dull noise comes from in front of me, but I can't register what it is. All I can do is focus on pulling rapid, sooty breaths into my heaving lungs. I'm exhausted from what little movement I've accomplished.

The world starts to come into focus as I catch my breath. Looking around at the destruction, I see a figure walking through the smoke towards me.

I watch the figure drawing closer before realizing that it's Neko. He's covered in ash and has a small cut on his face. It looks like he's got snow on him.

The surrounding sound sharpens and the ringing in my ears softens. Neko grabs my shoulders. "James. Hey, James! You're alright, I've got you. You were in an explosion. Where's Luke?" Neko looks around, looking for our missing teammate.

My brain must really be scrambled. I can't seem to focus on anything he's saying. His mouth moves, but the sound is delayed. I know he's talking to me, but nothing makes sense.

"James!" My wandering eyes snap back to Neko's smudged face. "Let's get you up and see if we can find Luke."

Luke?

Where is Luke? Was he nearby when the explosion happened?

"What…what exploded?" I barely manage to get the words out of my dry mouth as I cough, choking.

"One of the cars in the caravan. Dimitri got away, and Kiera took Hannah and Marcus."

"What?" I mumble as Neko helps me to my feet, careful not to jostle my injured arm. I feel like I'm on a boat in rocky waters. The world swims in and out of focus as I sway unsteadily on my feet.

"Take it slow, man." Neko has a tight grip on my upper arm and secures my injured arm in a makeshift sling.

When did he do that?

"Where's Luke?" I ask, suddenly overcome with overwhelming concern for the younger man.

"I don't know. I haven't seen him since the explosion."

I look around and see the corner where Luke stood earlier in the day when we were preparing for the caravan carrying Dimitri. I can't remember anything past seeing Luke give me a thumbs-up from across the street before the caravan came around the corner.

Pointing toward the blast-riddled building across the street, Neko helps me walk toward where I last saw Luke.

"Do you see him anywhere?" I choke out, still coughing around what feels like a swollen tongue.

Maybe I bit it when I was blown backward by the explosion.

Neko turns to answer me when I glimpse a booted foot underneath a pile of debris in front of us.

"Neko, there." My voice sounds oddly hollow and dead in my ears as I look at the dusty, scuffed boot. Visions of Shawn's bloody body slither through my blast-addled brain.

The laces are undone.

"Stay right here," Neko says, jogging to where the body lies buried under debris from the building and cars.

I can't stay here; I need to help.

I stumble forward, and with what little strength I have left, I help Neko remove the debris from the person beneath it. As we lift what looks to be the remains of a car's hood, I see Luke's blonde hair, and everything seems to freeze.

He looks like he's asleep.

Neko kneels over Luke, checking for a pulse before taking his belt off to make a tourniquet above a wound on his lower leg. As he tightens the belt, a gasp from Luke draws my eyes to his face and his bright, blue eyes find mine.

"James?"

"I'm here, Luke, I'm right here."

"What's going on?" Luke's raspy voice is barely audible above the sirens and screams echoing down the street.

"The caravan exploded," Neko repeats as he looks over Luke's wounds.

I'm suddenly lightheaded and my legs start to shake with exhaustion. I sit down roughly next to Luke, still heaving in breaths of ash-laden air into my aching chest as it settles around us.

"Are you okay?" Luke asks as Neko continues to look him over and triage his wounds.

I can't bring myself to talk, so I nod. I zone out, disconnecting, trying to stop the memories from returning. The thick, cloying stench of blood transports me back to holding Shawn's bloody body in my arms as he struggles to take a breath around the fluid filling his lungs.

A touch on my hand brings me back to reality. Luke is still lying on his back but has reached over and is tentatively holding onto my hand. I look from his blood and dust-covered face to our hands, trying to process what's happening.

Everything is still swimming. I think I might have blown an eardrum. I'm not fully aware of what's happening around me and am struggling to process everything.

Panic creeps into my gut. It takes hold of my already struggling lungs and turns my muscles into tightened ropes.

"James? James!" Luke tightens his hold on my hand, and I glance at him. His eyes are brighter than usual. The dark red of the blood and gray of the dust on his face make them pop against his paler skin.

"I asked if you were okay," Luke says again. I focus on his lips, trying to comprehend what he's saying.

My head feels cloudy and heavy. I must have hit it hard.

Nodding slowly, I lock eyes with Luke before glancing down at his prone body to where Neko is still working on his wounded leg. I can't bring myself to ask if Luke is okay.

"I'm fine," he says as if he can read my mind. "I'm fine, James. Take a deep breath, breathe." He squeezes my hand again and I draw a full breath, forcing it into my tight lungs. In through my nose, out through my mouth—just like they teach us in boot camp.

Nodding, I look away, unable to focus and take in the wreckage around us. The street has been cleared; all that remains are the remnants of the burnt-out cars and those caught in the explosion, Luke and I included.

Neko stands quickly, drawing my attention away from the destruction around us. He calls out and waves his arms above his head. I can barely hear what he's screaming, so I look to Luke to help me understand what's happening.

"The team is going to transport us to the hospital. Some of them went with Gray and Kee to deal with Kiera," Luke says, instinctively knowing what I'm asking.

Nodding, I feel the weight of my head as I move it. *Maybe I shouldn't be moving it so much.* I take my hand away from Luke's, slide it along the rubble-covered road, and bring it to my head. I feel along my scalp and find a large gash on the back that is leaking blood.

That'll do it.

I pull my hand away and look at it. Reality and the past blur together. I'm covered in the violent red of his blood as it spills from his body.

Is it Luke or Shawn lying motionless next to me?

The ringing in my ears morphs into the whizzing of bullets as gunfire rages around me. I'm unable to move, refusing to leave him as he dies in my arms.

His blue eyes lock on mine and I watch the light leave them. Dim, bluish-gray, sightless orbs left behind.

A hand on my shoulder snaps me out of it. Neko's face fills my vision. "James? Dude, you must be more fucked up than I thought. I need you to get up and walk for me. Can you do that?"

I muster the courage to look back to Luke, only to find that he's no longer there. I follow the trail of blood to one of the SUVs that's parked a few feet away.

"Come on, let's get you to the hospital, check your ears, and head out."

I let Neko help me, leaning on him to keep my balance as I stumble over charred car bits. He guides me to the back of the SUV where they've laid down the second row of seats, making enough room for Luke and me to lie down.

Neko crawls into the back of the SUV first while directing me to sit, then lean back into his arms. He pulls me back into the SUV with his hands under my armpits. I let out the breath I didn't know I was holding, suddenly overcome with sheer exhaustion. My eyelids feel so heavy and my chest aches with loss. I sink into the hard floor, focusing on the feeling of the rough carpet on my skin.

"You need to stay awake," Luke says.

Neko agrees as he shuts the door. "That's right, James. No sleeping. Stay awake. Luke, talk to him."

The door shuts and a few seconds later, we're bumping along the road to the hospital where Hannah works. We're there too often.

As if reading my thoughts, Luke says, "Do you think they get tired of seeing us at the hospital?"

I'm not sure if I can trust my voice, but I manage to croak a weak, "Yes." It's getting harder with the vehicle rocking and the white noise still filling my ears.

"Hey, James, you have to stay awake. You've probably got a nasty concussion." Luke reaches over and holds my hand again. I fight the urge to pull my hand away. Maybe Luke is feeling scared and needs some reassurance. I can do that for him. I can let him hold my hand. It doesn't mean anything else.

I breathe in through my nose and out through my mouth several times, dragging cold air into my parched lungs.

"Tell me something about yourself." Luke's voice softens, yet he tightens his grip on my hand.

"You first." I can't open my eyes without the world swimming and swirling around me. I definitely have a concussion, maybe the worst one I've ever experienced.

"Jesus, man, you are a fortress. Fine. I grew up in the south so when I first joined the Feather Flight Group, they made fun of my accent." A small groan escapes from Luke's tightly clenched lips, reminding me that he's also been hurt.

I turn my head tentatively and look at the man lying next to me in the back of the SUV. "Are you going to be okay?" I'm scared to ask. What if he's not, but thinks he is? What if Luke's injuries are worse than they seem?

His pale face is still covered in blood and soot, but the light is back in his blue eyes. His long, blonde hair is matted to his head in spots where he was hit with shrapnel, no longer in a man bun.

I try to raise my head to look at his leg, but can't. It's just so damn heavy.

"Your leg?" I manage.

"It'll be fine. I mean…I think it will be. It's pretty fucked up, kinda like your arm, but I think it'll be fine." There's trepidation in his voice. When I open my eyes again, he's looking down at his leg, uncertainty written across his face.

I squeeze his hand and he looks over, meeting my eyes.

"You still have to tell me something about yourself," Luke says, giving me one of his smirks.

How can he always be so positive?

Shawn was like that, too. So cheerful and…light.

Fuck, I can't think about Shawn. I haven't thought about him in so long, but today is dredging up all the memories and feelings that I've had safely buried for years.

The air in my lungs catches, and I feel like I'm choking for a second before I force the air out with a little hiccup. I'm panicking again—I know the feeling all too well. I try to control it with my breathing before it completely takes over.

"James?" Luke props himself up while looking at my face.

I close my eyes and concentrate on my breathing. I can't look at Luke, he reminds me too much of Shawn.

"I'm fine," I force out between my teeth.

"What's happening right now?" he asks, his hand leaving mine to settle on my shoulder.

"Nothing. Nothing is happening, I'm all good." I would roll away from him if I could, but the very thought of moving makes my body protest.

"You're not *all good*," Luke says, concern obvious in his tone.

"I'll be fine. I just need a minute to catch my breath."

"Did you break a rib or something?" He goes to feel my ribs.

"No, my ribs are fine. I just need a fucking minute, okay!" I can hear the frustration and anger in my voice, making me even more frustrated.

I take another deep breath. "I'm sorry, I'm just… I'm sorry. I didn't mean to snap." I slowly open my eyes, but Luke's look of hurt and my swimming head make me drop my gaze before I get sick.

"No worries, man. You do you." Luke settles back, removing his hand from my shoulder and laying it across his stomach, far from my hand. "I was only trying to help."

I stretch my fingers out as if I could catch his hand from where I'm lying, but I know I've pushed him away with my outburst. Luke is worried about me; I know I should appreciate his care. I'm aware of all of this, but I can't do anything when panic hits. It consumes me, taking over everything to where I can barely keep myself together. He was asking too many questions.

I feel like sobbing, letting the pressure in my chest loose and falling apart right here. But I don't. That's not the type of man I'm supposed to be. I'm not supposed to show emotions or weakness. I need to be strong.

I swallow my pain, panic, and feelings. I let the moments pass, trying not to feel bad, but knowing that I've fucked up.

CHAPTER 2

Luke

've been in pain before, but this might take the cake. My leg is on fire. The pain starts where the shrapnel hits and radiates out from there.

I can handle it, though. I need to stay aware and together for James' sake. He was closer to the blast and way more fucked up than I am. I can see the dullness in his brown eyes and that worries me. It's the same shell-shocked look I've seen in the eyes of teammates who have been through traumatic events. Something tells me it's not just what happened today that has James so shaken up.

He's got something else going on in his head that he's not ready to share. I don't know enough about him to say anything about it, but it's evident he's not prepared to open up.

Laying in the back I try not to close my eyes, but the desire to rest is overwhelming. I'd do about anything to get rid of the pain coursing through my body right now. James stretches out his hand as if he's searching for mine.

Do I hold his hand again?

I want to, but I'm worried I've already pushed him too far. What if that pushes him over the edge?

Fuck it. I've never been one to overthink things, why start now?

I take my hand from my stomach and reach out, lacing my fingers with his. The palm of my hand rests on the back of his hand. He doesn't pull away.

A sigh releases despite his tightly closed lips, and I see the tension in his shoulders lessen as they settle back against the SUV floor.

I guess it pays not to overthink.

As I settle, the vehicle stops and the back pops open. James immediately pulls his hand away from mine, lifting his head to look out before closing his eyes and laying it back down. His concussion has to be bad if it's impacting his vision that much. He's also got blood coming out of his right ear, so he's likely blown an eardrum. But it's the blood seeping through the bandage on his head that has me worried.

"Let's get you guys inside." It's Cassie, Hannah's friend, who's unfortunately had to deal with all of us before. Her long, dark hair is tied up in a messy ponytail and she looks tired. It must be a long shift.

"Take James first, I think he's worse off," I say, motioning toward James.

"I'm the doctor, Luke, and right now, your leg looks bad, so you go first. James will be right behind you."

I go to protest, but her no-bullshit look shuts me up. I let Neko and the nurses manhandle me, helping me out of the SUV.

"Jesus, guys, take it easy on me. I just got blown up," I mutter as they almost drop me while transferring me to a gurney.

Neko smiles and pats my shoulder. "Good to see you haven't lost your sense of humor."

"Never," I say back with a grin.

Cassie shakes her head. "Take Luke to curtain two and James to curtain four." Cassie is already turning towards James as I'm wheeled away.

"How ya doing, James?" I hear her ask him.

"Been better." His voice is soft and gruff. I hear his stifled groans as they move him out of the SUV.

I crane my head to see him, to make sure he's alright.

"He'll be fine," Neko says, giving me a knowing grin.

"Will you keep an eye on him for me?" I ask as they continue to wheel me into the ER.

"You got it. I have to get to Hannah, but Mika will be here with you, and I'll check in with you later," Neko says as he peels off from me and waits for James' gurney to come through the doors.

The rest of the night is blurry with doctors and nurses coming and going. The word *surgery* is whispered occasionally until Cassie finally comes in and officially gives me the news.

"Well, Luke, it looks like they're going to operate on your leg to repair the damage done by the shrapnel you took. You'll likely be in a boot or a cast once they're done. That also means physical therapy to fully get you back up and running."

I nod as she talks. This isn't my first rodeo with surgery or physical therapy. It's never fun, but it's a necessary evil. Mika demands that we keep ourselves in good mental and physical shape if we work with the Feather Flight Team. We need to have our shit together so that we can help others when we get the call. I've only been on a handful of rescue missions with the team, but I'll need to take care of myself if I want to remain with them. I'll do my physical therapy like the good boy I am and return to work promptly.

"Thanks, Cassie. I appreciate what you do here," I say, looking at the door as someone else walks past.

"How's everyone else doing?" I ask, thinking not only of James, but also of Hannah, Marcus, Kee, and Gray. I've heard from Mika that Kiera was killed in the rescue and that Hannah and Marcus made it out with minor injuries, but I still want to know more.

"They're shaken up, but everyone is recovering. Marcus had to get stitches, but everyone should be fine."

"What about James?" I hold my breath, waiting for her response.

Cassie gives me a soft smile as she shuffles through the papers in her hand. "James' arm is broken, and he's got a severe concussion. You know I shouldn't be telling you any of this though, right?"

"I appreciate it, Cassie. Thank you. What room is he in?"

"The room across the hall. Marcus is in the one just down the hall on the right. At this rate, we should designate a wing to you guys." Cassie chuckles softly.

"Thanks again for letting me know how everyone is doing."

"Get some rest." At that, Cassie leaves and shuts the door behind her.

I can rest a little easier now knowing that everyone is okay. I hate that Dimitri is still out there, but at least Kiera has been taken care of and James will be alright.

I've had a thing for James since I first saw him in Club Midnight. I'm a sucker for dark, brooding guys and James checks all my boxes. Not to mention he's fucking hot, especially with his slightly Greek features and olive skin. He's my type, but I wonder if I'm his. I don't usually pursue men whose sexual preferences I don't know, but with James, I can't help myself.

I'm not sure what or who James is into, and from my observations, it doesn't seem like anyone on his team is, either. The man is a fortress. He rarely shows emotion and always scowls, looking completely emotionless. It's impressive and kinda scary at the same time.

I have seen…moments of something between us, but not enough to feel comfortable making a move. There have been a few times I've caught him watching me. Then there was the ride here; holding his hand was electric. But I need to feel him out a bit more. I did see something in him today that I hadn't seen before—emotion.

Shifting, I try to alleviate some of the pain thrumming through my leg. The painkillers help, but I'm still uncomfortable. I hate lying here. It gives my brain time to wander.

I look at the closed door, wishing it was open so I could see James. I'm worried about him. He took a hell of a blow to the head and was so confused. Despite that, I still felt him seeking comfort from me.

He held my hand.

I wonder if he was aware he was doing that when we were lying in the rubble. I know he was once we got to the SUV, but he was lost in himself right after the explosion. His eyes glassed over and were far away. He was in another time.

I shift again, trying to get comfortable, when there's a soft knock on the door.

"Yeah!" I call out.

Mika opens the door a crack and pops his head in.

"Are you decent?" he jokes, giving me a huge smile.

"Hey! Yeah, get in here. I'm fucking dying for some company."

Mika comes in, followed closely by Neko who shuts the door behind them.

"How are you feeling, kid?" Mika has a habit of calling almost all of us *kids*. He's only forty, but apparently, that means the rest of us are children. He doesn't mean it in a demeaning way. Something about it brings me a sense of comfort, so I don't mind.

"I'm good… Fine. Cassie said I'll need surgery for my leg, so I'm waiting to hear more about that, but I'm confident I'll be able to bounce back quickly." I reach for Mika's extended hand as he gets closer.

"You had us all worried for a second. Neko said you looked like shit when they found you under the debris."

I give Neko a dirty look as he stands next to Mika. I don't need the boss to think I'm worse off than I am. Neko smirks back at me.

"I'm all good," I say with my most charming smile, squeezing his hand before dropping it.

"Y'all heard anything about James?" I ask, trying to hide how desperate I am regarding information about his well-being.

"Not too much, just that he's got one hell of a concussion, and his arm is pretty jacked up. I think they were saying he might need surgery as well, but I'm not sure." Neko pulls up a chair and settles next to me as he's talking.

"He was really out of it, wasn't he?" I whisper, looking at Neko. "I'm kind of worried about his mental health coming away from this."

"Why's that?" Mika asks.

"He had a familiar look in his eyes. He wasn't just shell-shocked, he was re-living something. He was lost in it for a moment," I say, looking between the two of them. The three of us exchange glances, knowing that we're all thinking about our own demons and PTSD.

"We will see how he's doing once he's awake. We can always

bring in Dr. Hardigan if he needs someone to talk to." Mika pats my shoulder and looks at Neko. "Let's give Luke some time to rest and go check up on Marcus."

"Tell Marcus I'm glad to hear that he's okay," I call out as the two of them walk to the door. "Don't be shy about visiting, either. I'm going to go crazy in here."

Neko smiles as he goes to close the door, before quickly popping his head back in.

"By the way, I saw you holding James' hand. Is there something going on there? You know the boss doesn't like us fraternizing with our clients."

"Dude, shut the fuck up and get out!" I shout at him, smiling as he tosses a wink and a wicked smile my way.

As silence fills the room, I'm left with my own thoughts again.

Today was close, really close. I got lucky today. If I'd been any nearer to the car...

I look down at my body, reminded that everything can change in a second. One second, I'm looking at James from across the road, giving him a thumbs up, and the next, I'm waking up to James and Neko pulling me out of the aftermath of an explosion.

Being near an explosion is always a surreal experience. Time stops for the briefest moment before speeding up at breakneck speeds. Going from one instance to the next while you're still trying to blink yourself back into existence. I've been in explosions before, but today was different.

When I was part of special reconnaissance operations overseas, gathering intelligence behind enemy lines, I had my small team with me for backup. I was not exposed like I was today on the street. I'm used to clandestine operations and sticking to the shadows, not standing on the corner of a street in broad daylight for anyone to take shots at. We should have planned our operation better, but given the time we had, we did what we could.

I put my arm over my eyes in an effort to stop my mind from running. I can't overthink it. It's already done. I can't go back and change anything.

My anxiety worsens the longer I'm left alone in bed, just thinking about all the things I could have, *should have*, done differently. The team relies on me, my recon, and my intelligence background; I feel like I let them down. I feel like James getting hurt is my fault. I stop staring out the window and turn to the bare room looking for something, *anything*, to take my mind off the explosion, off James. The nurses come in for another round of vitals before leaving me alone again. The sound of the clock ticking is the only sound in the room besides my breathing.

There's a soft knock at the door. I open my eyes as the door slowly opens.

Kee walks in looking like shit. But then again, I think we all do after what we've been through today.

"Hey, how're you doing?" she asks, stepping fully into the room.

"Hey," I say softly, giving her a thumbs-up and a full-wattage smile as she sits next to the bed.

"I just wanted to stop by and say thanks for what you did for James today. I tried to see him earlier, but the nurses aren't letting any of us in until he's more aware of his surroundings. I guess he's still out of it."

"I would do it for anyone, Kee, and James helped me a lot today as well. I need to thank him, too."

Kee nods, looks down at her hands, and softly says, "I don't know a lot about James, but I do know that he's been through some heavy shit. He was a Marine Force Recon and did a lot of dangerous, wild things. I think that's why he's so closed off."

"James was in the Marines?" I ask, surprised.

I figured he was in some branch of the military but hadn't spent too much time thinking about it.

Kee chuckles. "Yeah, he doesn't speak about it a lot. I actually only think he's mentioned it once. When he became my partner, they gave me a fast and dirty rundown of his credentials. But I wanted to talk to you because I know you're…curious about him, based on that favor you asked of me on our way to Moscow. I think James is into you as well. He seems unsettled around you, which is weird for him, and I've seen him watching you a few times. That being said, I think you should take it slow. I don't think James is used to people pursuing him…romantically." Kee finishes that last sentence with a small smile as she looks up at me.

"Don't worry, Kee. I'll go easy on him. My priority is to make sure that he's okay after what happened today. My feelings for him won't interfere with that, I promise." I smile back at her.

"Just take it slow and be careful with him. He's more delicate than I think either of us knows."

"I'll do my best, Kee. I want nothing more than to be a friend to James first. If something can grow from that, great. But if that's where we stay, that's where we stay. I won't push him."

"Good, I'm going to hold you to that." Kee genuinely smiles as she pushes back from the bed and stands up.

"You'll be here for a while with him, anyway, as you both heal. It'll be good for him to have someone besides me around."

I nod as she turns and walks towards the door. "Hey! If you see James before me, could you let him know that I'm alright and that I'm just across the hall?" I know he probably doesn't care, but something in me wants him to know.

"I'll pass it along to him. Now get some rest!" Kee shuts the door behind her as she leaves. I settle down into the hospital bed and close my eyes.

Now that the place is quiet and it's too late for any more visitors today, exhaustion sets in. I didn't even realize that I was this tired. My thoughts wander back to holding James' hand. I struggle to keep my eyes open as the pain medication slinks through my veins, leaving a warm, fuzzy trail of oblivion behind it.

CHAPTER 3

James

've been asleep for a long time; I can tell by the way my back and body feel. I'm comfortable but sore. My arm aches, but it doesn't necessarily *hurt*. Somewhere in my mind, I know that's because I'm probably on some pain medication. I move my fingers and toes. They all seem to work, even the fingers of my broken arm.

I'm alive.

For a moment after the explosion, I questioned whether I made it or not. It had all seemed like a dream, the way the world was swimming and everything moved so slowly.

Luke.

I open my eyes at the thought of him and look around the room. It's a standard hospital room that's completely empty beside me. *Good.* I'm not ready to deal with anyone yet. I need to get my shit together and figure out what happened. I can remember most of the day up to the explosion and some of what occurred afterward, but it's blurry.

I remember finding Luke, though. I remember how he looked

lying in the rubble, covered in dust and blood. How his ocean-blue eyes sparkled in the dim light when he woke up.

He woke up. He was awake.

My stilted breath comes rushing out of my body and I gasp for another.

He's fine.

I look at the stand next to my bed where there's some water along with a small notepad. I recognize Kee's handwriting immediately with its smooth, flowing cursive. Grunting, I reach for the notepad.

> *You're alive! They wouldn't let us stay all night, but*
> *I wanted to let you know that Luke is fine; he's in*
> *the room across the hall. I'll be by tomorrow during*
> *visiting hours. ~K*

A small bit of the tension in my chest and shoulders lessens at Kee's note. Luke must be alright if he's across the hall and not in the intensive care unit. We both managed to make it out of the explosion in one piece... Mostly.

I'm drained from the little movement I've made. Looking at the clock, I see that it's about two in the morning. I put the note on the stand and lay back down, letting my body's heaviness sink into the lumpy hospital mattress.

I'm drifting off to sleep when the first pings of panic hit me. It starts small, a kernel in the back of my mind. A simple thought of, *What if Luke had died?* And it expands from there, spiraling out like a drop of water in a lake. Memories flood the darkness behind my eyelids.

Shawn turns to give the all-clear, the sound of the RPG ripping through the air toward us. I couldn't move or call out to him fast enough for him to move in time. Everything hits me. The feeling of the gravel crunching under my boots as I run towards the explosion. The smell of copper and fire. The bright red of his blood against the charred ground. Shawn's dulling eyes as he looks up at me.

Flooded by the memories, I sit up in a panic and can't seem to catch my breath.

Fuck.

I bring my left hand to my chest and press, trying to convince my body to relax and draw in a full breath, but it won't. I can't.

I can't breathe.

More panic floods me as I can't catch my breath. The little machine next to my bed is going crazy, chiming repeatedly. As I look at it, the red lines start to blur. Darkness edges the corners of my vision.

Suddenly, there are people around me. People I don't know. The panic worsens as their hands press and pull on my body, trying to get me to lay back. An oxygen mask is forced over my face and there are hands holding me down.

"You must calm down! Mr. Adamo! James! Can you hear me? You need to calm down. You're having a panic attack." The nurse is talking loudly and calmly. I know it's supposed to help, but it doesn't. It reminds me of when I was in the hospital after Shawn's death. Of the time before I had control.

I can't go back to that place. I can't go back to not being in control. *I won't.*

Panic squeezes my chest, and I hear myself groan as the little machine grows louder.

"What's going on?" a new voice cuts in, and a clean-shaven, young man's face appears at the edge of the bed.

"Panic attack, I think. Can't get him to calm down."

"Mr. Adamo, I'm going to give you a mild sedative to help you calm down, okay?" The doctor gives the nurse an order and moments later a needle is inserted into my port, delivering the medication.

Sluggishness caresses my nerves as it moves through my body. The panic rears its head at the imposter in my body and I squeeze my eyes shut, willing my body to calm down. Willing the visions of Shawn's broken body to go away. I need it to stop. I can't bear seeing him bleed out anymore. I can't survive this again.

I draw a deep, ragged breath as the medication wins the battle over my body and mind. I draw another as my head swims in the drug, letting the heaviness take over my body.

"Keep an eye on him and check every couple of hours to see how he's sleeping. Put him in for a psych consult as well, will you?" The doctor's warped, slow voice drips through my consciousness like honey running down the outside of a jar.

I don't remember falling asleep.

The light coming in from the window catches my attention. The clock reads ten in the morning. Good. I needed the rest and luckily, I didn't have any nightmares. I don't want them to come back. I might be able to handle panic attacks, but post-traumatic nightmares are a different beast.

Shifting in the bed, I push myself up with my good arm and into a fully seated position. Leaning over, I grab the glass of water and take a sip. I doubt anyone has been by this morning, but now that I'm starting to wake up and the drugs are wearing off, the thought of having to deal with people makes my skin crawl.

I just want to be left alone.

As if the universe is mocking me, there's a knock at the door. The doctor walks in followed by two nurses.

"Good morning, Mr. Adamo. It's good to see you up. How are you feeling?"

"Fine," I reply, setting the water down.

"Good to hear. So, you had a panic attack last night. A pretty severe one, if you remember it. We had to sedate you. Have you had panic attacks before?"

"Yes."

Keep it short and sweet; don't give them more information than they need.

"Did you receive treatment for them?"

"Yes."

It's none of your business.

"I'm going to recommend that you see someone for them."

"Great."

Fuck off.

The doctor raises his eyebrows realizing that I'm not going to say anything further on the topic, so he pivots.

"We've put a cast on your arm. You were lucky; we were able to set it, and it should heal fine with the cast. You are also concussed, but those symptoms should pass. Do you have any questions?"

"No."

Not my first rodeo.

"Alright, well, we recommend you stay here at least another night to see how you do. In the meantime, your friend across the hall has been asking about you, so we're going to see about moving you to the same room."

I can't handle being close to Luke.

"Please, that's not necessary."

"Oh, it's no problem at all. Let us know if you need anything." The doctor waves on his way out. He was way too friendly for my liking. Give me a surly Marine medic any day over whatever the hell that just was.

Within thirty minutes, the nurses transport my bed, wheeling me into the empty room across the hall.

"Where's Luke?" I ask the nurse behind me at the head of the bed.

"In surgery, I think. He should be done soon." They push my bed against the opposite wall and ensure everything is set up before leaving me in peace.

I've just started to doze off when the room door opens and another bed is brought in. Luke isn't awake yet. His leg is elevated and bandaged. They don't say anything to me as they drop him off, the room filling with the sounds of his soft breaths.

I haven't seen him since the SUV and find myself mesmerized by the way he looks as he sleeps. His brow is slightly furrowed as if he's thinking about something in his sleep. He has a light dusting of golden hair along his jaw, as his facial hair starts to grow in after days of not shaving. He has several cuts and bruises that mar his skin. Under different circumstances you would think he was taking a nap. He seems to be resting peacefully, which is more than I can say for myself.

I didn't want to be moved into the same room due to the nightmares. The last thing I want is to scream myself awake and subject Luke to that. I haven't done that in a while, but the explosion brings up a lot of things I thought I had buried long ago.

Sighing in resignation, I lay back and try not to think about the nightmares, the panic, or Luke. He's so hard to ignore, though.

My eyes drift back over to his sleeping figure across the room. I wonder how the surgery went.

I don't really know what to make of Luke. He confuses me. I've caught him looking at me a few times in a way that I recognize as something more than curiosity. Hell, I've caught *myself* looking at him in a similar way. I know he's talked to Kee about me. If I had to guess, I would say he might be into me, but that doesn't make any sense.

Why would he be into me?

He knows nothing about me.

"Whatcha thinking about?" His voice is soft, raspy, and sleepy, breaking me from my thoughts.

This is what he would sound like waking up in bed.

I shake my head, bringing my eyes up to meet Luke's drowsy ones. The blue of them shocking my system, as always.

"Nothing," I mutter, shifting under his sleepy gaze.

I feel like he can see right through me with his crystal blue eyes. What if he figures out that I'm broken?

"How are you feeling?" I ask, deciding to warm up to him a bit.

"Like I was blown up." Luke shifts under his blanket as if he's going to try and sit up.

"Maybe you should take it slow. Your leg's suspended, so I don't know if you can sit up or not." A ping of concern bounces through my skull.

I must have really hit my head hard.

Groaning, Luke stops his struggle and flops back on his pillow. "That might be a good idea."

"Are you okay?" he asks sleepily, his voice barely audible in the quiet room. His eyes are shut, and he seems to be drifting in and out of sleep as he talks to me.

"Yeah, I'm alright. Just a little banged up," I say as his face goes soft and his breathing evens out. He's asleep again.

Looking out the window at the wintery mix coming down, I'm reminded of how the ash looked after the explosion. Floating silently through the darkened sky.

Shaking my head to prevent myself from thinking back on the caravan, I try to focus on something else. Except there's nothing to look at; there's only Luke, conveniently laid up across from me.

I don't know anything about him other than he's great at gathering intelligence, worked at Club Midnight as a doorman, and is also a member of the Feather Flight Team. Other than that, he's a mystery. It's weird—I know more about what he does for a living than his normal, everyday life.

A small voice in my head whispers, *"He's kind, funny, good-looking, has a great smile, beautiful eyes, and a fantastic body."*
What the fuck?
Think about something else. Anything else.

Okay, so we know Dimitri got away. Where would he go? There's no way he's going to let any of us get away with killing his daughter, Kiera. He's bound to come back at us with something. Will he return to Russia like she did to gather his men? Will he stay here and mount an attack?

We should probably move Hannah out of her house and to a safe location. We should have done that initially, but we wanted her to have some sense of normalcy. We tried to keep her safe, but also let her live her life. Was that the right choice? Would Marcus and Hannah not have been taken hostage again if we had played our hands differently?
Focus, James.

Dimitri isn't Kiera. He already has the manpower here in town, he won't need to leave. He'll be able to make moves faster than Kiera did. We need to move Hannah, *fast*. Her father, District Attorney Winters, should also be placed in protective custody. There's no telling what Dimitri will do.

I look around the room for my cell phone, but there's nothing but the landline phone on the table next to my bed.

Grunting with effort, I lean over, grab it off the hook, and dial Kee's cell number.

"Hello?" Her voice immediately eases some of the tension wrapping around my muscles.

"Kee? It's James."

"James? What the hell? What are you doing?" Kee sounds angry and concerned that I'm calling her.

"Kee, we need to relocate Hannah soon. She won't be safe at her house and neither will we."

"James, you should be resting."

"I will. I need to know that everyone is safe and that we're thinking about Dimitri's next move."

"We are. We're already talking about where we're going to relocate. We're on it. I promise." Hearing Kee say that alleviates more tension and worry.

"Will you keep me in the loop?"

"Of course. I'll be by later today to update you, but you should really be resting."

"I will, I promise."

"Alright, I'll see you later. And stop worrying," Kee chides as she hangs up the phone.

"She's right, you should stop worrying." Luke's gruff voice fills the room from across the small space that divides us.

"I thought you were sleeping."

"Someone talks loudly."

"Shit, sorry." I go to run my hand through my hair only to be reminded that my head is bandaged.

Luke chuckles as he watches me struggle. "It's okay. I think I'll be in and out of sleep a lot today. Why aren't you resting?"

"I..." *Do I tell him that I don't want to sleep because I'll wake both of us up screaming?* "Um, I'm not tired. I got a lot of sleep last night and I'm not on any heavy meds, so I want to stay as aware as possible," I overexplain in my sad attempt at hiding the truth.

"I see."

He knows. He must know that I'm lying.

"Well, you don't have to worry about snoring or anything. I can usually sleep through anything." Luke gives me a smile that makes my stomach jump.

"Didn't you just say I woke you up by me talking?"

Luke grins at me from his bed and shrugs his shoulders as if that explains everything.

"Seriously though, James, you should rest. I have a feeling this is going to be the only downtime we have in a while with Dimitri coming after us." Luke's smile slips from his face and his sunshiny demeanor turns serious, just like it did when we were in Russia.

"You're right," I say, nodding in agreement as Luke closes his eyes again and sinks into his bed.

I follow suit, hoping that my nightmares stay away just a little longer.

CHAPTER 4

Luke

James has been asleep for a long time, but his sleep doesn't look restful. He tosses, and turns, and occasionally cries out, waking me up in the process.

I'm not supposed to get up and walk just yet, but I'm tempted to go over and see if I can wake him. I know from personal experience with nightmares related to my deployments that I would want someone to wake me up if I were in one. I sit up in my bed and start to remove my leg from the sling that it's suspended in, when James cries out and shoots up in bed.

James immediately grabs his head and folds over himself as if he's in pain.

"James?" I ask softly from across the room. "Are you alright?"

It takes him a moment to respond. I can see his shoulders heaving as he catches his breath. He sniffles and pulls himself upright, letting go of his head and quickly wiping his eyes and face.

"Yeah, sorry. I'm sorry. I was afraid this would happen." His sleep-flushed cheeks redden more as he avoids looking at me.

"It's okay. Was it a nightmare?"

"Uh, yeah, yeah, it was. It was…a dream about something that happened a long time ago." James rubs his face again and flops back onto his pillow.

I'm still trying to get my leg out of the sling while trying to be as casual as possible. I don't want to rush him or make him feel like he has to tell me. "Wanna talk about it?"

"Not really." James has one arm thrown over his eyes with his arm cast resting across his stomach. I watch him, drawing in a breath and hoping he'll open up to me.

"It's just… The explosion has brought some stuff up that I thought I had dealt with years ago."

I stay quiet, patiently waiting for James to continue. He's looking down at his hands, picking at the edge of his cast.

"I lost someone really close to me about ten years ago and this whole situation has me scrambling." James sighs and rubs his forearm across his eyes.

"I'm fucking frustrated that it's coming back. I really thought I had my shit together."

I've finally freed my leg and flop back onto my own pillow, taking a deep breath and pausing before I reply.

"It happens to the best of us, man. I've had to work hard to manage a lot of my anxiety around providing support from a distance for the team because of an incident when I was a special reconnaissance operator."

Staring at the ceiling, I think about the last time this happened during our search for Marcus. Luckily, Hannah was there. Having another person around helped me keep it together. When things heated up in our pursuit of Kiera, I was able to breathe through it and keep moving forward.

"Do you ever have panic attacks?" James' voice is barely audible, I strain to hear what he's saying.

"Panic attacks? I don't think I've had like a *full-on* panic attack, but sometimes my anxiety gets to me, and I lose my shit. I yell at other people for being incompetent. I know it's getting bad when the slightest thing, like someone bumping into me, sets me off. I've gotten a handle on it, but every now and then, I lose control."

"I have panic attacks."

James' admission is barely a whisper, and I sit up to hear him better, wincing in pain. He's in the same position, with his arm over his eyes. He's hiding, but I don't mind. If it helps him talk, he can do whatever he needs to.

"Are they bad?" I ask in a hushed voice.

"Yeah…" His voice breaks and his heartbeat on the monitor speeds up. "I feel like someone is squeezing my lungs and heart. I can't breathe and sometimes…I black out."

"Sounds kinda scary." I want to comfort James, to wrap my arms around him, but I'm trapped in this damn hospital bed. All I can do is watch as he curls into himself.

"*Scary* is one word for it, *fucked* is another." He wipes his face again, lowering his arm and looking out the window at the gray world outside. I follow James' eyes to the bank of windows. It's snowing again. The world outside isn't much brighter than the mood inside.

"How do you deal with the panic attacks?" I'm desperate to keep him talking. This is the most he's ever said; the fact that he's sharing so much is shocking.

"I used to go to therapy for it: for the panic, the anxiety, the nightmares, all of it. I haven't been in a long time because I haven't had any issues. But…now, I don't know. Everything's been thrown off. It's coming back." James looks from the window down to his cast and picks at it again.

"I'm not sure if I can go through all of this again."

His voice has gotten softer and my palms itch with the need to comfort him. What would he do if I did? Would he let me?

"James…I—"

The door swings open before I can finish my thought and our doctor walks in.

"Gentlemen, I have good news! You're both going home today." I glance over at James and am not surprised to see that his walls are up again. His guard is up, masking his anxiety and his fears. James already has his legs over the edge of the bed and is looking around for his clothes.

"Easy, Mr. Adamo. You'll need someone to pick you up. I don't want you driving just yet with your concussion. But everything else looks good. Just be sure to take it easy for the next week."

"Right," James mutters, reaching for the hospital phone on the table next to his bed.

"Now you, Mr. Weber, we're going to bring in a walking boot for you. You'll need to keep an eye on the incision and change your bandages regularly. You should really be on crutches, but I know you don't want to go that route. You're also going to need a ride out of here."

"Thanks, Doc," I say, holding out my hand for a shake.

"My pleasure." As he turns, he looks at James, walking closer to where he sits perched on the edge of the mattress. He whispers just loud enough that I can hear what he says.

"Oh, and Mr. Adamo, I've put a referral in for a mental health evaluation. Be sure to follow up after they call you."

James nods, his eyes darting past the doctor to where I sit.

"Good luck to you both!" the doctor calls on his way out of the room.

"I can practically taste our freedom." I look across to James and give him a wicked smile, trying to lighten the mood.

To my surprise, he returns it. "Kee and Mika are on their way here to get us. We're almost out of here."

James seems different. He's still a cloud of grumpiness, but something about him seems more human than before. He doesn't seem as stoic or emotionless as he was before. Am I seeing the real James now?

I smile back at him as he sits, bouncing one of his legs on the linoleum floor. A few moments later, a nurse comes in with my boot and helps me get situated after changing my bandages and checking the other cuts on my body. I catch James watching as she removes the bandages on my leg before he turns away, looking down at his hands and fiddling with his cast again.

I wonder what he's thinking about. I think I saw a flash of sadness cross his face before he looked away.

Just as the nurse is heading out, Mika and Kee arrive.

"We're here to bust the two of you out!" Kee shouts as she strolls into the room.

"Oh, thank God. Did you bring some clothes?" James asks, standing up and holding his gown closed behind him.

"Yup, I've got ya covered, partner." Kee hands over a bag and James edges his way to the bathroom to get changed.

"Here's your shit," Mika says with a smile, tossing a bag of clothes on the bed next to me.

"Thanks. Y'all mind stepping out so I can get changed?"

"What can't I watch?" Kee jokes before leaving the room.

Mika lingers for a moment. "You all good?" he asks.

I can see the concern in his weary face. I know that he's asking because he cares about all the people under his command.

"Yeah, I'm all good. I should be in this boot for a while and then I'll hit physical therapy hard."

"Alright, don't push yourself too hard." Mika leaves and I get to my feet. I'm a bit unsteady as I get used to the boot and experiment putting weight on it. Pain laces up my shin and calf, making me gasp and lean into the bed for support.

I'm still leaning against the edge of the bed, catching my breath, when James comes out of the bathroom. He's dressed in dark jeans that hug his muscular thighs and ass with a dark blue, knit sweater.

Holy shit.

"You alright?" he asks, walking towards me quickly.

"Just a bit unbalanced, is all." In more than one way. James strides forward and grabs hold of my arm.

"Here, lean on me."

I lean into his sturdy body and try putting pressure on my leg again. I'm briefly distracted from my pain by the feel of his hard muscles flexing under my arm as he holds me up.

"Shit. I think I might need those crutches after all. I'm in more pain than I thought I would be."

James looks up from my foot to my face, we're mere inches apart. His brown eyes are flecked with gold and green.

"Right, let me get them," he mutters, his eyes moving from my eyes and lingering on my lips before he glances quickly at my eyes again.

I can't fully comprehend what just happened.

Before I can do anything about it, James is halfway to the

door. He pokes his head out and talks quietly and quickly to some-one, probably Kee or Mika, about getting me crutches. His grip on the door frame is tight. Once he's done asking for the crutches, he does something I'm not expecting.

He shuts the door and comes back to me, taking my arm, putting it over his shoulder, and looking at me again.

"Are you going to get dressed, or do you want to wear this gown out of here?" he asks gruffly.

"Right, can you pass me my pants?" I suddenly feel a little shy, which is not me. It's a weird feeling; I'm not quite sure what to do with myself. I've always been confident and go for what and who I want, but this is…unsettling.

James reaches out with his injured arm and hooks my pants out of the bag with his fingertips.

"This is pathetic," I say as he hands them to me while I wobble on my good leg.

"Well, between the two of us, we have a fully functioning body."

"James, did you make a joke?" I pause, looking up at him with half of my good leg in my pants.

He rolls his eyes as he looks down at me.

"Sit down," he suddenly huffs out, helping me over to the edge of the bed. "If you tell anyone I helped you with this, I'll kill you." Now, he's all business. I have to say, this is the first time I've had someone help me put my pants *on* instead of taking them off.

James gets my pants on my good leg and looks at my boot. "Well, we can either cut your pant leg off or take your boot off, put the pants on, and then put the boot back on. Your pants are too damn tight to fit over the boot."

"People usually like my tight pants," I say, making his head snap up. It's not lost on either of us that he's kneeling between my legs right now.

I arch an eyebrow at him, and he quickly looks back to my leg.

"Stop joking around. What do you want to do?"

"Let's cut the pant leg off," I say, letting him off easy.

"Alright, give me a second." James gets back up and goes to the door again. I know he's talking to Mika this time as he returns with a small blade. Mika insists on carrying it even though it's not the best for hand-to-hand combat.

James takes the pants and, holding them away from my leg, makes quick, decisive, and effective cuts.

I loved these jeans.

I say a quick, mental *thank you* to my favorite pair of jeans as James tosses the remnants of their lower half to the side. He's cut them just below the knee, nodding as he looks up at me expectantly.

The angle at which he's looking at me makes his eyes seem wider, the embodiment of puppy dog eyes. I mentally slap myself before I can reach out and stroke the side of his face, but *damn*, seeing him like this on his knees does something for me.

This is what he would look like with my cock in his mouth. Wanting to please me.

James says something.

"What?"

"Lift your leg," he says again as we both pretend to *not notice* the growing bulge under my hospital gown.

He maneuvers the cut pant leg around my boot, and I stand up, leaning on him again to pull the pants up.

"I think you can manage your own shirt," he mutters as he turns his back to me and walks towards the door.

"Thank you!" I call after him. I can't help but chuckle at myself for getting riled up over James—*James!*—of all people. I slip out of the gown, letting it drop to the floor, and pull a T-shirt and hoodie out of the bag that Mika has brought for me.

"Hey, do you—" James' voice cuts off and I turn around to see him looking at me with a funny expression on his face.

My scars.

I give him a sheepish grin, my stomach fluttering knowing that he's looking at me. "It's not my first time being blown up."

He blinks, looks at me, then *looks* at me. I watch as his whiskey eyes roam over my body, taking in every inch of my face, chest, abs, and waist. He snaps his eyes back to my face, his own reddening with the knowledge that he just blatantly checked me out.

"I have to go," James says, swinging the door open and rushing out.

"Dude, why the rush?" I hear Kee call after him.

Mika pokes his head in and shakes it as he sees my half-dressed state.

"What did you do, Luke?"

"Nothing! Honestly, I didn't do anything this time. I swear!" I finish pulling my shirt over my head, followed by my hoodie. Mika walks in, holding my new pair of crutches.

"Let's get outta here."

Mika hands me the crutches and I easily keep pace with him as we leave the hospital. It's not my first time on crutches, either.

I wave to the nurses as I hobble out of the doors, hearing giggles behind me as we make our way out of the hospital.

"Do you ever get tired of it?"

"Tired of what?" I ask, looking at Mika while trying not to eat shit on the icy pavement.

"Being incorrigible?"

"Mika, you know you can't use big words around me." Smiling, I hop up into his truck, making sure not to hit my leg on the way in.

"Shut up and put your seat belt on. We're going to the compound and the roads that far out of town are shit."

"The compound? Why are you taking me there? Can't you drop me off at my house? I can manage on my own."

"The whole team is at the compound, including Finn. He was released from the hospital a few days ago and we've got Neko to look after him. I want everyone at the compound until we're done dealing with Dimitri."

"What about Hannah, Gray, and the rest of the team?"

"I spoke with Gray and Kee today, they're going to move out to the compound as well. Probably tomorrow or the day after. Hannah has to get things in order before she can leave."

"That's good. I wish we could move everyone out there right now instead of waiting."

"Yeah, it's not ideal, but we've got extra eyes on the house in the meantime."

"Okay, can you drop me by my house first so I can grab my things?"

"Yeah, I guess I can do that. You want me to wait for you?"

"No, I'm going to go over to Hannah's, and I'll hitch a ride with them when they head out. An extra set of eyes won't hurt." I look out the window, contemplating whether my plan is going to work.

"What are you planning?" Mika asks, not taking his eyes off the road. *Shit, he knows me too well.*

"Nothing. I want to make sure I'm there for Marcus and

Gray if they need anything. I'll come out to the compound when they do."

Mika cuts a glance at me. "I don't know if I believe you."

"I'll be good, boss. I promise." I shoot him a grin and turn back to look out the window.

I wouldn't say I like lying, but the truth is that I'm going to *try* and be good. I shouldn't be held responsible for what I do around James. His presence drives me a little crazy, those damn amber eyes of his.

I look up as we pull into my driveway. It's hard to see from the main road outside of town, but Mika knows it well, easily finding and turning onto the shoddily paved back road.

The road is deceiving, and most people turn around before they reach the break in the tree-lined area. I can't help but smile as we break out of the trees into a large clearing where my house stands waiting for me. It's a traditional white farmhouse with a large wrap-around porch. I've missed home. I'm not quite sure how long it's been since I've been here, given that I've been staying at Hannah's during this whole situation. When I'm not there, I'm at my place in the compound.

"Good to be home?" Mika asks.

"So damn good," I say, opening the truck door.

"You gonna be able to get out of here on your own?" he asks again.

"Mika, I've got it handled."

"If you say so, man. Give me a holler if you need anything."

"Copy." I slam the door to the truck as I get my crutches under me and start up the snow-dusted front walkway.

This house has been in my family since the early 1900's. I had to fight my parents to keep it and then again when I wanted to purchase it from them. They would have given it to me, but I insisted on buying the old property and fixing the place up. It was the perfect project for me to tackle when I got out of the military.

I hop up the four front steps and crutch my way to the front door, unlocking it and walking into the impressive foyer. Stopping, I take in the vaulted ceilings with the Tiffany glass chandelier. Sighing, I drop my keys in the basket where they belong and make my way through my house.

It's dark and a little dank as no one has been in it for at least a couple of months—at least not for any extended period. I'm tempted to lie down on my couch for a quick nap, but I fight the urge. I've got a mission. *James*. I can't get his eyes and the way he looked at me out of my head. I want him to look at me like that again…and again.

I shake myself from my thoughts; I need to focus. I also have another mission: the safety of my friends and team. I've got my own plan for keeping them safe—I have no doubt that James has a similar one. He's likely gone home to gather some things before heading over to Hannah's. I need to catch him before he makes the move. I have something I need to say to him.

I grab my go-bag from the downstairs closet and then make my way up the stairs to my room. I'm lucky in that I can easily navigate my house on crutches because I have used them for extended periods of time before. The last time I was in an explosion, I ended up on crutches for several weeks.

I grab my other duffle from my bedroom closet and toss random clothes and toiletries into it.

Going down the stairs is a lot more challenging than going up. I end up tossing my bag down to the first landing and following behind it slowly. Once I've made it to the bottom floor, I grab both of my bags, sling them over my shoulder, and make my way out to the garage.

I know I shouldn't drive, but I also know I can manage it independently. It's my left foot anyway, so it's fine, right?

My truck starts easily, and I reverse out of the garage, closing it behind me and heading towards the main road.

I only have one thing on my mind, and I won't be content until I've addressed that need.

CHAPTER 5

James

"James, wait up!" Kee shouts as she follows behind me. I'm practically sprinting out of the hospital.

I need to get away from Luke. I can't be near him a moment longer.

I rush through the door into the city's brisk, wintery mix of February.

"James, for God's sake, slow down!" Kee runs to catch up to me and grabs my good arm.

"What is going on?" Concern makes her eyes darken as she looks at me.

"I just had to get out of there."

"Why, what's happened?" Kee grabs my arm again as I go to walk away. "Hey, you can talk to me."

"I don't like hospitals, and I don't like being cooped up in a room with Luke. He talks too much." My mind is racing with what I should and shouldn't tell her.

I didn't tell our employer about my PTSD. The last thing I need is for Kee to let it slip or act weird around me. I know she wouldn't tell our boss on purpose, but sometimes she gets to talking or joking around, saying things she shouldn't.

"I know that's not all. I mean, you practically ran out of there."

"Can you take me to my place?"

"Of course I can, James. But we're partners and I need you to remember that. You can count on me. I'm here for you."

"Thanks, Kee. I appreciate it. I'll let you know if I need anything." I want to tell her. Shit, it'd be nice to open up to Kee. I'm nervous, though. I can't have her treating me differently. I can't have her knowing about Shawn. I don't want her pity.

"James …" Kee squeezes my arm. I know she's going to say something that I can't handle right now.

"Let's go." I brush past her and head toward the SUV parked next to a large truck. The last thing I want is to hurt Kee's feelings, but I don't want to stay here any longer and risk Luke catching up with me.

I step up to the passenger side door and wait for her to unlock it. Kee reluctantly unlocks the door and follows my lead.

"Will you be staying at your place?" she asks, getting in the vehicle.

"No, I figured I'd go to Hannah's in case you need extra backup."

"Do you need me to wait for you at your place?"

"No, I can get a ride to Hannah's."

We're pulling up to my apartment complex before I know it, and for a brief moment, I wonder if I've fallen asleep on the drive.

"James, we're here."

Clearing my throat, I turn and give her a tight grin. "Thanks, Kee. I'll text you when I'm on my way over."

Kee nods and I open the door, sliding out and striding toward the complex's door.

My apartment complex was built in the mid-seventies. Some aspects of it have yet to be updated, including the security system at the front of the building. I easily slip through the unlocked front doors and make my way to the elevator. It must be my lucky day, because it's actually working today and not out of service like it normally is.

Stepping out of the elevator, I walk down the hallway, the smell of various foods assaulting my nostrils as it mixes with the smell of dank carpet from the hall. I don't particularly appreciate living here, but it's cheap and serves its purpose. It's a place to store my shit and to sleep—that's all I need. I like to keep my life as minimal and simple as possible, and my place reflects that.

I unlock my door and step into my bare living space. It's a simple one-bedroom apartment with windows on the outside wall, letting in an absorbent amount of sunlight. It's the best part about the place unless I'm trying to sleep in.

I walk directly to the bedroom and pull out my go-bag. I have pretty much everything I need in here but decide to throw in some extra clothes and gear, including my Ka-Bar knife and SIG Sauer P320 MHS. I throw extra magazines in next to my socks and zip up the bag.

I've only been home for about fifteen minutes and I'm not exactly dying to get to Hannah's. I go to my small kitchen and grab a beer from the fridge. I'm pretty sure I'm not supposed to be drinking, but what the hell, who's going to stop me?

Opening my beer, I sit on the only piece of furniture in my small apartment: the couch.

My arm is throbbing. I know a better choice would be to take a pain pill, but I don't like taking medication if I don't absolutely need it. I need to sit and relax for a moment before diving back into the chaos at Hannah's place.

The silence of my apartment surrounds me. Something that once brought me comfort now makes my skin crawl and my mind race. I keep seeing Luke lying in the rubble, looking peaceful in his unconsciousness yet surrounded by destruction, covered in soot and blood. Thinking of Luke makes me think of Shawn; how they looked so similar as I held Shawn in my arms during his last moments.

My unease grows and I feel slightly dizzy. Putting my beer down on the floor, I rub my eyes and start to stand. Drinking isn't going to help—it's a bad idea anyway.

The knock at my apartment door makes me jump, causing me to pause. I pull my gun and walk over to the door. Holding the gun and opening the door with the same hand is a bitch, but I manage. To my surprise, Luke is standing there.

He's using his crutches and leaning on his good side to avoid putting pressure on his booted leg. *Why is he here?* I open the door, looking the younger man up and down. I can't help but be caught up in his charming smile and blue eyes.

"What are you doing here?" I ask.

Luke takes one unbalanced step into my apartment, grabs my face in his hands, and roughly kisses me.

Shock makes me freeze and it takes me a moment to fully process what the hell is going on. When my brain catches up, I lean into the kiss. Luke's lips are soft and his beard is scratchy. He smells like cedar and burning wood. I get lost in the heady scent of him before catching myself and pulling away abruptly.

"What the fuck, Luke!"

He hobbles backward and gathers his crutches, not breaking eye contact with me.

"I'll see you at Hannah's," he says a bit breathlessly as he turns and crutches down the hallway toward the elevator.

I lean out of my door and watch him go.

I don't know how to feel about what just happened. I don't think I hated it, but I don't think I enjoyed it, either. It isn't my first time kissing a man, but it's my first time kissing someone since Shawn and that means something to me. Luke doesn't look back once as he makes his way to the elevator at the end of the hallway. I can't seem to pull my eyes away from his back.

Holy shit. I think I enjoyed that. I can still taste him on my lips and my heart is still beating wildly in my chest. I can't seem to catch my breath.

I duck back into my apartment and shut the door, leaning my forehead against it as it shuts quietly.

This is bad—this is so bad.

There are so many things wrong with this situation. One, it's Luke. I barely know him, and I don't know if I can handle his sunny disposition. Two, we're kind of working together. Three, I can't go through anything remotely close to what happened with Shawn. I won't survive losing someone again.

Pushing away from the door, I move back to the couch and flop down, staring up at the plain white ceiling.

How do I navigate this?

Running my hands through my hair around the bandage, I can't help but think about the last time *someone else* ran their hands through my hair. It was Shawn, the night before he died. We would sneak into each other's rooms on base.

Being secretive was a part of the job and we were pretty good at it, but the guys on our team were trained to be perceptive, too. I'm sure everyone knew about us, but no one ever said anything.

Our unit was close, and out of respect for one another, we stayed out of each other's business. Some of the guys did treat Shawn and I like we were "*less than*".

Shawn wasn't like the others, though. He cared a lot about all of us. It was this softness that drew me to him. He loved everyone on the team and made sure that the guys were doing well. I had never had anyone care for me like that before, it made me want to be vulnerable and open with him.

When he died, I completely spiraled. If they didn't know before, they did after. I was inconsolable, depressed—and riddled with anxiety and survivor's guilt. I still am. I'm just a little better at managing it. At least, I was.

Luke has managed to ease his way into my mind. He did it so slowly and subtly that I didn't even realize it until the explosion when I saw him lying there. It hit me harder than I comprehended. Seeing him like that and how similar he looked to Shawn, it's really fucking with my mind.

Leaning forward, resting my elbow on my knee and holding my head in my hand, I can't stop thinking about Luke and Shawn and all their similarities. Not only in how they look with their blonde hair and blue eyes, but also in how they act. Luke is more playful, more boyish than Shawn, but Shawn had that same spark in his eye, like he was up to no good. They both care about the people around them more than themselves.

I can't believe I'm doing this again.

I shake my head as if I could knock some sense into myself.

It would be disastrous to start anything with Luke. It would be complicated and could get messy. Who knows how long this thing with Dimitri is going to last? What if Luke's looking for something quick and fun, done with me when everything goes back to normal?

The pit in my stomach grows as I think about Luke more. I'm not sure how to handle this.

My phone vibrates in my pocket.

Hey, just checking in. It's been a minute since I dropped you off. Are you still coming to Hannah's?

Kee's message spurs me into action. I can't avoid Luke forever, so I might as well bite the bullet and get over there.

I'm on my way, sorry to make you worry.

I grab my bag and head out the door, ordering a car on my way out of my apartment.

It's all going to be good. Pretend like nothing has happened. Keep your walls up and your wits about you.

I keep repeating this on the way to Hannah's. It's a short drive and I'm there in front of her townhouse in Olde Town before I know it.

I step out of the vehicle and am met by two of Mika's guys.

"Oh, hey, James. How are you doing?" John asks while eyeballing the street behind me. His tone is casual, but everything about John screams business. He's not messing around.

"Good, I'm just checking in," I say as they move to the side, letting me up the stairs to Hannah's.

Given everything going on, it's good to see that security has been heightened. The quicker we move to the compound, the better.

Opening the front door, I step into the foyer and pause, trying to determine where Kee and the others are. I can hear voices coming from the kitchen and the sunroom. I head toward the sunroom at the back of the house. It's Hannah's favorite spot; always a good bet that she'll be there.

Walking past the kitchen, I catch pieces of the conversation between Mika and Marcus.

"I think we should relocate tonight." Mika sounds set in his suggestion, his tone not leaving much room for negotiations, but it seems like Marcus will try.

"I agree, but Hannah says she needs one more night here to get things sorted at work."

"I don't like it, Marcus. I've got a bad feeling."

"I know. I do, too. But you know how Hannah gets. She's determined to stay here."

The conversation stops momentarily before continuing after I've gone past. Their voices fade as I walk to the back room.

"James!" Hannah's exclaim pulls me from my wandering thoughts. Hannah's in her usual jeans and an oversized sweater that looks like it might be one of Gray's. Her strawberry blonde hair is down, falling in loose curls just below her shoulders. If it weren't for the worry lines between her eyebrows, you wouldn't know that anything wrong was going on.

I give a tight smile and I see the shock on her face briefly before a big smile replaces it.

"I was starting to get worried," Kee whispers to me.

I give her a nod. "No need to worry. I was moving a little slow."

Hannah moves forward and wraps me in a hug before I can protest. As she's hugging me, I look over her shoulder and make eye contact with the one person I'm dying to avoid.

Luke is here.

Of course, he is. Where else would he be? Plus, he said he would see me at Hannah's. My denial had me hoping that he wouldn't be here.

"James," he says with a slight smirk.

"Luke," I respond, pulling back from Hannah's hug and scratching the back of my head where the stitches stretch.

"How are you?" Hannah's eyes are full of worry.

I'm getting tired of people asking me that question. "Fine."

Hannah nods and doesn't press me. She knows I'm not one for a lot of words, so she moves to sit back down next to Gray on the small couch that's a newer addition to the sunroom. Gray gives me a nod and doesn't press with questions or conversation. They know that I'm on the quiet side and don't push me to be something I'm not.

As I nod back to Gray, I notice the dark smudges under their eyes and the way they keep one hand on Hannah. The latest events are messing with all of us.

"So, what's the plan?" I ask as casually as possible, putting my good hand in my pocket. I'm still in my jeans and sweater, not bothering to change into my suit. I notice that Kee isn't dressed in her suit, either. We all seem to have gotten too comfortable around each other.

The lines are getting too blurry for my liking.

"We're looking to relocate first thing in the morning. Hannah has a few things to wrap up for the hospital before going on extended leave. So, we can focus on finding Dimitri and dealing with him, knowing that everyone is safe in the compound," Gray says, looking around the room from face to face.

I think we should move quicker, but I keep that to myself. "Sounds good," I say instead.

Kee looks at me, shocked, as does Gray. "You're not going to argue that we should move tonight?" Kee asks, looking around the room in utter shock.

"I'm sure you've already heard that from a few folks," I reply, pulling up a chair and sitting down, suddenly exhausted. My head is pounding and I'm not sure if it's from the few sips of beer I had or from the concussion.

"You really must have a bad concussion," Kee jokes, patting my shoulder.

Another tight smile.

"Do you need me to do anything?" I ask, looking from Kee, to Gray, then risking a glance in Luke's direction.

"Why don't you join me on surveillance duty in the kitchen?" Luke suggests.

Before I can respond, he moves towards me with his crutches, arching a golden eyebrow as he passes.

"Sure," I mutter, following his shadowy form to the kitchen.

As Luke and I walk in, Mika and Marcus leave us to go check in on Hannah and the others in the sunroom.

"Sit," Luke demands, pointing to the chair next to his.

My stomach flips. I swallow before pulling the chair out and taking my place at the table next to him.

"You look like shit," he says softly.

I look sideways at him, at the bruises on his face, neck, arms, and hands. He's covered in them.

"So do you," I reply.

"How's your arm feeling?"

"It…isn't great. What about your leg?"

"It's been better."

I nod, looking at the computer screens in front of me and the camera angles around the premises.

"We should leave tonight," I whisper.

"I know. I tried to tell Hannah that, but she's stubborn as hell, as you know."

Nodding again, I shift in my seat. My body hurts and sitting makes it worse. I would do anything to lay down right now and rest. Reaching up, I fiddle with the strap of my sling, trying to get it to not rub on the skin of my neck.

Before I can sort it out, Luke is leaning into my space, reaching his arms around my neck. Our faces are a few inches apart. He smells of vetiver, moss, and burning wood. I freeze as his thumbs gently glide past the exposed skin on my neck. Chills race through my body.

"There," he whispers softly, fixing the strap.

CHAPTER 6

Luke

Everything in my body is urging me on. Urging me to kiss James again. I know I can't, though, especially with so many people around. But damn, do I want to.

I'm inches away from his plump lips and can't help but look at them as I slowly pull away. I fully expect him to be jumpy, but James doesn't move away first. The opposite happens. He doesn't move at all. He lets me fix his sling and doesn't flinch when I touch him. Maybe James is into me, too?

I pull back, smile at him, and blink, breaking the spell we were under.

James clears his throat, his hand absently touching the places on his neck that I touched before adjusting the sling one last time. He settles back into his chair and stares at the computer screens in front of us.

Turning away from him, I run my hand through my long, blonde hair. I pull it free from the bun that it's in before pulling it back and securing it in a tighter one. James watches my every move.

His eyes. He's giving me those wide, bewildered eyes again. The darkening of the whiskey color makes the computer light bounce off the golden embers swimming in the amber depths.

I am in so much trouble.

It's my turn to clear my throat as I struggle to stay composed. The house seems warmer, and I tug on my hoodie to cool myself down. James watches my every move and his breathing quickens. I shift, trying to get comfortable around my arousal.

I need to distract myself.

"Tell me something about yourself, James." I don't look directly at him, but I keep staring at the screens in front of us, trying desperately not to feel his eyes lingering on my face. He slowly pulls them away to focus on the security footage.

"What do you want to know?" he whispers.

"How long were you in the military?"

"Ten years, the Marines. You?" James shifts in his seat, visibly uncomfortable with the conversation.

"Special reconnaissance operator for eight years." The familiar feeling of excitement races through my body and makes my legs bounce just thinking about the missions we went on.

"Did you enjoy the work, all the secret operations?" James looks at me again.

"Yeah, I really enjoyed it. I loved the team even more." I can't keep the smile off my face as I think about my old unit and how I get to share them with James.

"Were any of the guys from Feather Flight Group a part of your old team?"

"No, most of my old teammates aren't around anymore."

"Shit. Sorry, Luke." James looks at me and then down at his hands. "I know what that's like."

I don't say anything. I want to give him the time he needs to continue if he wants to. Give him space.

"I…most of…my team died on an operation. It was an explosion." I didn't think it was possible, but James' voice became softer. He's still looking down at his hands and I fight the urge to reach over and wrap his hands in mine.

"You don't have to tell me more than you're ready to." I keep my eyes on the screens, not trying to pressure him.

"A really good friend died on that operation. Shawn was his name." I steal a glance at James to see that he's picking at the skin around his nails while his leg bounces. He's radiating anxiety. I wish there were a way for me to make it better, to make it stop.

"I somehow made it out."

"James." He won't look at me.

"James, you know it's not your fault, right? It's not your fault that you survived."

"I've heard that a lot. I know I'm not responsible, but it doesn't stop the nightmares or the guilt."

"If you're interested, we have a therapist at the compound. Maybe you could talk to her about it. She might be able to help you out, especially with the anxiety."

"What anxiety?" James scoffs in a sad attempt to lighten the mood.

I can't stop myself any longer and I reach for his bouncing leg, placing my hand just above his knee.

"This anxiety." He looks at me with his sad, brown eyes and my breath catches.

"Everything good in here?" Gray asks, walking in.

I pull away from James, straightening and looking at Gray.

"All good here," I say.

Gray looks between us. "You sure?"

"We're good," James says.

"Okay…" Gray walks backward slowly, keeping their eye on us. Their apprehension is palpable as they leave the room.

James and I have sat in silence for what feels like hours, but it's actually only been one. It's not uncomfortable silence; rather, it feels like we're two old friends sitting in comfort, enjoying each other's company. It's new for me. I'm usually the one talking all the time, but James' presence is calming, even though he is definitely not calm internally.

James tries to hide his anxiety, but it's obvious if you look closely at him. The leg that bounces every now and then. The picking at the skin around his fingers. The way he bites the inside of his cheek. The flexing of the muscle in his defined jaw. Even the way he watches the monitors, eyes shifting constantly. It all screams anxiety.

"I'll be right back," James says, suddenly rising from his chair. He runs his hand down his pants.

As he starts down the hall, the first call comes in over the radio.

"Everyone on alert. There's a caravan of SUVs heading your way. They're three blocks away and it looks suspicious as fuck." Dalton's voice carries through the radio as the entire house holds its breath.

"Everyone up, grab your bags, and let's head out the back door," I shout, scrambling up from the kitchen table and grabbing my crutches.

James is next to me as I hobble to the hallway where our bags are. He grabs our bags and stays next to me as we make our way to the sunroom and backdoor. Hannah, Gray, Kee, and Marcus are already waiting for us.

Gray reaches for my bag and James lets them take it, wincing slightly as it jostles his broken arm.

"Let's go, stay low and follow me closely," Gray says, looking each of us in the eyes before moving toward the back door.

"If you're not moving, you need to get your asses in gear." Dalton's voice is rushed, his huffing over the radio letting us know he's on the move.

Gray is at the front and James is bringing up the rear. He sticks close to me and occasionally puts out his good arm to help me balance as I slip on the snow-slicked ground.

It's fucking impossible to move quickly and quietly while on crutches and I'm pissed that I have to use them. There's nothing I can do now but grit my teeth against the pain and keep moving.

We pop out on the opposite side of the block where we've stashed our vehicles. The sound of running feet draws my attention and Dalton rounds the corner a few seconds later.

"How close?" I ask.

"They're pretty much on us. We need to move now."

We pile into our vehicles, and I find myself in a truck with James, just the two of us, as Dalton rides with Hannah and Gray. Marcus and Kee take their own vehicle and we all drive away from the house.

The plan is to head off in various directions in case we're followed and to meet up at the compound once we've lost our tails. James is driving, which makes me nuts especially with only one arm, but I suppose that's better than driving with one leg.

We take off down the street, leaving the rest of the group behind. As we round the corner, I look to the side and see several men, all in black, heading up to Hannah's door. Before we can turn, I see one of them point in our direction.

"*Fuck.* Punch it, James."

"Right."

James takes off down the road, making several random turns in the hopes of misleading and losing the three SUVs now racing after us.

"I'm sorry, I shouldn't have stopped."

"It's fine, James. Keep up the turns and speed. We will lose them soon."

"Copy."

James presses on the gas and the truck bucks as we take off, racing down the freshly plowed roads throughout Hannah's neighborhood.

"Let's hit the interstate and get out of here."

James makes several deft turns and we're soon speeding up the on-ramp for the interstate. We've managed to ditch two of the SUVs, but one is still on our asses and doesn't seem to be slowing down their pursuit.

"What's the plan?" James asks, glancing into the rearview mirror.

Gunfire ricochets off the back of the truck. A bullet strikes the glass of the back window, causing it to fracture but not break.

"Shit," James whispers but doesn't falter or take his eyes off the road.

"If we can't shake them, our best bet is to outrun them and hope we can get to the compound before they run us off the road."

"Right." James checks the mirrors and pushes down on the gas again, inching us forward but not losing the SUV behind us.

Another series of gunshots hit the vehicle, making us both hunker down behind our seats.

"Should we return fire?" James asks, swerving around traffic and punching the gas.

"No, I don't want to risk hitting a civilian vehicle." Glancing behind us, we've gained a few car lengths.

"Take the next exit then take a left at the stoplight. Run it if you have to."

"Copy." James is in military mode, which is helpful. It's a language we both understand and we can act on instinct, which will keep us alive.

James takes the exit at breakneck speed and barely touches his brakes as he slides through the intersection. He narrowly misses an oncoming car before straightening out and taking off down the side road. Thank God it's a bit icy out.

We've got some distance now.

"Keep going and then turn right at the third light."

James blows through the next three lights and makes the turn.

"I think we're clear," I say, turning around in my seat and looking out the window to verify.

The truck slows a bit as James loosens his grip on the wheel.

"You drive pretty well for having only one arm." I can't help but smile as I look at James across the cab of the truck.

"That was too close for my liking," he says, glancing behind us again. "Where to from here?"

"Stay on this road for about two miles. The compound turn will be on the right and you'll be able to see the gates about a mile after we turn."

"Okay." James keeps up his speed, but not enough to make us a target for local law enforcement in the area.

"There's the turn."

As James turns, I catch movement out of my periphery and have barely enough time to throw up my arm before the SUV crashes into the side of our truck.

Darkness rushes to meet me as my head bounces off the windowpane.

CHAPTER 7
James

The black SUV slams into the truck's passenger side, tilting us onto two wheels before we skid into the ditch and continue the roll.

I glance over, hear Luke grunt, and see him limply hanging in his seat as the truck tumbles. There's blood on the window where he hit his head.

Shit, this is bad. Moving once we're free of the truck is going to be damn near impossible.

The truck comes to a stop upside down. I immediately reach for my seatbelt while unsuccessfully trying to brace myself with my cast.

I fall unceremoniously to the roof of the truck and reach for Luke's belt, dropping him down as well. I don't have time to care if it hurts him, we need to move.

I ditch my sling, grab Luke under his arms, and crawl backward out of the truck's driver's side window, which faces the woods surrounding the dirt country road. Luke doesn't make a sound or stir as I pull him, his large frame almost not fitting through the broken-out window.

Ducking down to stay hidden behind the truck, I pause to listen. I don't hear anyone from the SUV. Grabbing Luke under his arms again, I drag him towards the trees. Maybe we can distance ourselves from them before they come around.

Breaking into the tree line, I prop Luke up against a cold trunk of the nearest tree and glance around it, trying to get a visual of our pursuers.

Their SUV sits idling on the side of the road, the front of it smashed from the impact with our truck. I can see two figures sitting in it. They aren't moving to get out, though.

Maybe they're shaken up by the impact?

"Luke…Luke!" I try to wake him up by slapping his face lightly and shaking his shoulders. I can't carry him, so I'll need him to move on his own.

Shaking him some more seems to do the job as his eyes open slowly, the bright blue dimmed some by his confusion. It doesn't last long, though. Luke comes fully awake and aware of his surroundings within seconds.

"Easy, you hit your head," I whisper, looking around the tree again. There's movement in the car.

"We need to get moving. Can you get up?" I take his arm with my good one and help him up. Luke leans on me for balance and tries putting his weight on his booted leg.

"Fuck, I don't think I can walk on it yet," he whispers, leaning into me more.

"It's fine, we can navigate that. I just need you to be somewhat mobile. Which way to the compound?" Every word out of my mouth leaves small clouds behind. The cold is starting to work its way through my sweater.

"That way." Luke points to our left and I tighten my arm

around his back as we move in that direction. It will be hard traveling through the snow with his leg, but we don't have any other choice.

The sound of doors closing behind us spurs me on and we move faster. Luke puts a little weight on his booted leg to help us move quicker. I can tell by the tension in his body against mine and the ticking in his jaw muscles that he's in a lot of pain, but we can deal with the pain and the consequences later. It's better than being dead.

"We need to move a bit quicker," I say, gripping Luke's waist tighter and holding him against my side to help alleviate some of the weight he's putting on his leg.

"Doing the best I can," he mumbles between grunts.

"How far is it?"

"Probably about a mile, maybe half a mile, through the woods. We should pop out close to the front gates."

"Christ, we may have to make a stand." I glance behind us and see two men in black at the tree line. We haven't made it far and it won't take them long to catch up to us.

"Do you have your phone?"

Luke pats his pockets, retrieving his phone from a front pant pocket.

"Can you call the team? Maybe they can help us out a bit?" We're both panting as we navigate through the snowy underbrush of the woods.

"I barely have a signal. I'll try a text, maybe it'll go through."

"Let 'em know we'll be coming in hot if we make it out of the woods."

I pause, holding onto Luke long enough to haul my ass over a fallen tree. Reaching back, Luke sits on the tree, swinging both legs over. I'm there helping him over it and back up as we set off again through the trees.

I can hear the crunch of their boots behind us and know they're close without turning to look. They aren't shooting, though, so they must need us alive.

I stumble over a hidden tree limb and almost take both of us down, but we somehow manage to stay on our feet and keep moving forward through the trees.

"I can see the road!" Luke exclaims breathlessly. I instinctively tighten my grip on him and move him closer so we can move faster.

We're almost there.

The sound of racing footsteps makes me glance behind us.

Shit.

I let go of Luke.

"What are you doing?" he asks, pausing to look at me.

"Go, I'll buy you some time."

Luke stops, leaning on a tree for balance.

"Luke, go!" I turn and start toward the two men running after us. I risk a glance back to ensure he's moving before returning to the task at hand.

I'm not a match for them in my current state, but I can slow them down enough to give Luke time to get to the road. Hopefully, the team will be there to meet him. I'll also be able to move quicker without him to get away from Dimitri's goons.

I duck down, dodging the first punch coming my way and grab the guy around the waist, using our momentum to tip us over into the snow. It knocks the breath out of him, and I pop up quickly to grab the second guy as he tries to run past to get to Luke.

Grabbing him by the back of his coat, I yank hard, throwing him off balance. He turns, swinging wildly and catching me in the jaw. Stars burst behind my eyelids and I stumble back a step, almost tripping over the first guy who's still getting back on his feet.

Dimitri's man in front of me grabs me by the collar, hauling me towards him as the guy behind me gets up.

Shit, this isn't going well.

I risk a glance in the direction Luke was going. I don't see him anymore, which is good. I hope he gets to the road.

I brace for the first punch as his fist connects with my stomach, forcing the air from my lungs.

Doubling over, I feign the need to drop to my knees. As the man holding onto me from behind bends over me, I quickly snap up and crush his nose with the back of my head. His grip loosens and I use my backward momentum to throw us back again. We stumble apart and I leave him to fumble with his broken nose as goon number two comes at me again. I need to make quick work of him so I can make my get away.

He comes at me swinging and I raise both arms to block the blow. His fist bounces off my cast and he recoils in pain. I lash out, catching him in the temple with a fist. He stumbles to the left and that's all the room I need.

I take off, racing through the snow and following Luke's uneven footsteps. I can't be that far behind him.

The trees ahead of me appear to thin.

I burst out of the trees to find a row of well-armed men pointing their weapons at me.

"Fuck, James. We almost shot you."

I bend over, resting my hand on my knee, attempting to catch my breath as Mika comes forward. Luke is leaning against one of the vehicles that is not far away.

"Let's get the hell outta here before your friends find their way out of the woods," Mika says, patting my heaving shoulder. Nodding, I stand up and walk with him towards the truck that Luke is leaning against.

"Get in, you two."

I slide into the back seat beside Luke, still catching my breath.

"Thanks," he says, giving me a small smile. His blonde hair has come loose from its bun and brushes the top of his muscular shoulders. He's got a small cut on the side of his head where it hit the glass, but other than that, he looks okay.

Correction. He looks gorgeous.

The exertion of running makes his cheeks rosy and the cold brings extra color to his pink lips. I'm overcome with the urge to wrap my hand in his hair at the base of his neck and pull him in for a kiss. My palms itch with the desire and need to do so.

Instead, I nod. "Of course." I give him a small smile in return and close my eyes, turning away from him and leaning against the window to concentrate on breathing.

"You're okay, right?"

"Just gotta catch my breath." My leg starts to bounce as the adrenaline wears off and the anxiety hits.

Luke's large hand is on my thigh, right above my knee, squeezing gently. It's weird, but soothing. My leg stops bouncing shortly after he places his hand on it. The warmth bleeds through the denim of my pants into my chilled flesh.

My mind stops spinning and I focus on the warmth of his hand on my cold leg. I want to hold his hand so badly. But there are too many people in the truck with us and I'm also confused. I have no idea what's going on between us or where exactly Luke stands with whatever the hell this is.

"Did everyone else make it to the compound?" I ask once I've caught my breath and have my wits about me.

"Yeah. When you weren't right behind them, we assumed something had happened and started driving back towards the road. That's when we got the text from Luke."

"Thank God it went through; otherwise, we might have been in trouble." I lean my warm face against the window and watch as the trees stream by.

The longer Luke's hand is on my leg, the less it bothers me. It's comforting. I glance at his reflection in the window, noting that he has his head back and his eyes closed.

"Hey," I reach and touch his hand that's placed on me, "you should probably stay awake since you hit your head."

"Mmmm…right." He opens his bleary eyes and turns his head towards me, glancing quickly at our hands that are resting together on my leg.

Neither of us says anything, but he squeezes lightly, and I instinctively squeeze his hand back.

What are we doing?

I look back at Luke and his eyes are closed again, but this time, his head is turned towards me, and I have a moment to take him in. He already has a bruise forming on the side of his face that hit the window. I let him rest with his eyes closed for a few minutes before grasping his hand again to wake him.

His eyes open just like they did after the explosion and for a moment, I'm back there, sitting next to his still body, surrounded by debris and ash. Blinking, I swallow and look forward. I take my hand from his and immediately regretting it, missing the feel of his flesh on mine, the warmth, the steadying feeling that it lends me.

"We're here," Dalton says. I look out the window and have to stop my jaw from falling open.

The fence around the place is fucking impressive. It's a massive, steel paneled gate with spikes on top, similar to the ones around the Capitol in D.C.

The fence goes on for what looks like miles and a small communication box is at the front of the gate. As the first car in our line pulls up, Mika types into the keypad at the front of the gate and the gate slowly swings outward towards the vehicles, revealing a dirt road towards more trees.

"Holy shit, what kind of compound is this?" I can't keep the awe out of my voice as we proceed down the dirt road and a series of brick buildings come into view.

"Impressive, isn't it?" Luke says, finally removing his hand from my thigh as we approach the brick buildings.

"Yeah, what have they been doing out here? This is some serious shit." I climb from the truck, feeling the tension and soreness in my muscles and still recovering from the earlier escape through the woods.

"Welcome to your new home for the next couple of weeks," Mika says, opening the door to the first building.

"This is where we monitor everything. There are more houses down the road where you'll be staying," he continues.

It's nothing but high-tech gear and electronics for as far as the eye can see. The place is currently empty, probably because we had to pull everyone away from monitoring the compound to come to rescue us.

As we continue through the front room, we enter their war room.

"This is where we do all of our planning and hold team meetings." Mika continues walking, sitting at the table to look at Luke and me.

"I know you must be tired after what happened today, so I'll keep this short. There's a good chance Dimitri knows where the compound is now because of what just happened. If he doesn't, it won't take him long to figure it out. We need to prepare. We've been monitoring the shipping yards, so we know he's got a lot of men with him, and he's brought in some heavy artillery."

Mika pauses, looking from Luke, to me, and then back to Luke, who reaches up to touch the blood trickling from the side of his head. I follow Mika's gaze. "Shouldn't he see a doctor or something?" I ask, nodding toward Luke.

Mika looks back at me and says, "He can handle a few more minutes. The living situation here is a little hectic right now and many houses further down the road are already occupied. We had to make some adjustments. Luke's house is the farthest down the road and right now, it is empty. So, James, you're going to be staying with Luke. Any objections?"

I barely have time to think about it before Luke answers, "No, he doesn't have any objections. It will be fine. I have more than enough space."

"Good, it's settled then. You'll be happy to know that I've stocked the place for you. Let's get you over to Neko so he can look at your head. James, we'll take you over to Luke's." Mika stands, slapping his leg as he does so, and gives us both a smile.

"Hopefully, you gents can get along!"

"I think getting along is the least of our concerns," I mutter as I follow the group out of the room.

I don't know the men at the computers monitoring the surrounding roads and compound, but I'm getting a better idea of just how well-prepared the Feather Flight Group is seeing as this entire compound is covered with cameras.

We're back in the truck, stopping momentarily to let Luke out at one of the smaller buildings set back from the others.

"I'll see you in a few. Help yourself to whatever's in the house," he says, hoping out of the truck.

Neko is there to meet him and help him into the medical center. Mika and I head towards the end of the dirt road, passing several modest houses on the way there.

"When did you start building this?" I ask, looking around in awe.

"Several years ago. When we got the team together, we found it was easier if we all lived in the same area. Then it progressed from there, to living here at the compound together."

"Smart. Does the entire team live here?"

"No, Luke doesn't live here full-time. He has his own house, but he lives here when we're on mission. A few other team members do the same, but Finn, Neko, Dalton, and I all live here full-time. This is Luke's place. Gray and Hannah are next door with me and Kee and Marcus are up the street at Neko's. Stop by if you need anything. Luke shouldn't be with Neko for long."

"Thanks, I should be fine. I appreciate you letting us stay here while we deal with Dimitri."

"Of course. Oh, and one more thing, Luke can sometimes be bold, so if you need your space, don't be afraid to tell him."

"What do you mean, *bold*?" I can feel a bit of heat touching my cheeks at what I think Mika is implying.

"Let's just say when Luke likes someone, it's easy to tell."

"You think Luke…likes me?" The heat in my cheeks intensifies, just saying the words out loud.

Laughing, Mika puts the truck in drive. "James, I have known Luke for years and I've never seen him look at someone like he looks at you. Keep your wits about you, my friend!"

Mika is still chuckling as he drives away, leaving me at Luke's doorstep.

Does everyone know that Luke has a thing for me?

I try the knob of the door and it opens easily, swinging inward and revealing a moderate, but rustic home. It's got the most up-to-date appliances, but the décor is comfortingly outdoorsy. It smells like cedar, which makes sense as I look up and see the large cedar beams across the vaulted ceiling. It's a beautiful home, not what I would expect from Luke. But then again, I don't know Luke well, so everything's a surprise.

I haul my bag farther into the house to the living room where several dark leather couches are situated around a fireplace, the brick from it reaching from the floor to the ceiling. I drop my bag next to the closest couch and sit down, all the energy and adrenaline leaving my body as soon as my ass hits the cushion.

I'm fucking exhausted and my arm is starting to beat in time with my heart. I grab the bottle of pills that the doctor prescribed me, pop two, and swallow them dry, not wanting to get up again.

The fuzzy feeling slinks through my veins after about thirty minutes. I feel my muscles relax, and the pain in my arm becomes a dull throb. I grab one of the throw pillows close to me and lay down on the couch, letting myself sink into it and relaxing into the pull of the drugs.

As the sun sets outside, I can't keep my eyes open, and soon, sleep claims me.

CHAPTER 8

Luke

've been at the medical center for way longer than I've wanted. But after making sure I'm not concussed and haven't broken anything in my face, Neko finally lets me go.

"Give me a ride to my place?" I ask as I walk out of the building.

"You got it. James is staying with you, right?" Neko gives me a look as we approach his truck.

"Yeah, made sense to have him stay with me since everyone is already bunked up. What's going on with you and Finn?" I counter, trying to stir the pot a bit and take the pressure off James and me.

Neko chuckles. "You're an asshole, ya know that? And whatever is going on between Finn and I is none of your damn business."

"Likewise with James and me. If you need to know something, I'll let you know."

Neko raises his brows and looks at me from the driver's side. "Getting a little pissy, are we?"

I shrug my shoulder and push the door open as we come to a

stop outside my house. Dim light comes from the front window. I shut the truck door, giving Neko the finger as he waggles his brows at me. I grab my bag from the back and head up the steps of the house.

As I open the door, I expect to see James sitting at the table or in the living room. What I'm not expecting is to see him sound asleep on the couch. I pause just inside the door before shutting it as quietly as possible behind me. I drop my bag next to the door and walk forward after slipping my shoe off.

James looks pale and tired even as he sleeps, with dark smudges under his eyes that mix with various shades of bruising. He's resting his broken arm across his stomach and is snoring lightly. There's a bottle of prescription pain medication on the end table.

I'm sure he was hurting after hauling my ass through the woods. I look down at my boot. I've lost my crutches during the chase today and will have to manage without them. Neko gave me something for my pain before I left the medical center.

I give James another look before limping over to the kitchen. I'm starving. I pull out some bacon and eggs; there's nothing better than breakfast for dinner. As I start to cook, the smell of sizzling bacon and fried eggs fills the house. I hear the telltale sound of someone moving on leather and know that James is stirring in the other room.

"Luke?" he groggily calls out from the living room.

"Yeah, I'm in the kitchen. Do you want some food?" I call out, only to look over and find him standing in the doorway.

"Oh, hey. Did you sleep well?" I ask, flipping the eggs and bacon over while plating others.

"Yeah, I was out. How long have you been back?"

"I just got here. You looked comfortable. Why don't you go

sit down and I'll bring you a plate when it's ready?" I look at him and freeze. He's combing his hand through his hair, his eyes are shut, and for a moment, he looks completely relaxed. I don't think he has any idea how attractive he is.

The smell of burning bacon turns my attention back to cooking. "Shit, I hope you like your bacon crispy."

"Actually, I do. I prefer it a little burnt."

"Perfect, this plate will be yours." I drop several pieces of bacon and several eggs on a plate.

I hand James the plate along with some silverware. "What do you want to drink? There's pretty much everything in the fridge."

"Water is fine." James walks to the dining room table, sets his plate down, and returns to fill a glass with water.

I track him as he moves around my house. It's like he's meant to be here. He seems to know where everything is and moves through the space with confidence and ease.

I finish cooking the rest of the bacon and eggs, bringing my plate and a plate of extra food to the table. I sit down across from James as he digs into his food.

"I didn't realize how hungry I was," he says quietly between bites. "Thank you for cooking."

"James."

He looks at me with those eyes from across the table and my confidence wavers.

"Yeah?"

"I…was wondering if you could tell me more about your teammate, Shawn."

James freezes with a forkful of egg halfway to his mouth. "What?"

"You mentioned that you guys were close when he died. I was

wondering if you would want to tell me about him and share a bit about him. Sometimes that can help."

There are a few beats of silence before he speaks. "I don't know if I'm ready to talk about Shawn. There was a lot between us. A lot of things happened and then he was killed right in front of me. I don't know if I *can* share."

I see James closing in on himself even as he's talking to me.

"Don't do that."

"What?"

"Shut down. It's okay if you don't want to talk about it, although I think it would help some to do so. I won't push you, but please don't shut down. I feel like you're finally starting to open up a little bit and let people in."

"Keeping people at arm's length makes it easier."

"How?"

"If I don't let people in and if something happens to them, it won't impact me as much. It will be easier to recover from it. Especially if it's someone like Kee, someone I'm around all the time."

"That's no way to live, James. Kee is the one person you should be the closest to. You two are partners. You should have an unbreakable bond."

"I can't do that." James repeatedly shakes his head, vehemently opposing what I'm saying.

"Just consider it. You don't have to make any decisions right now or anything, but just think about it."

"Is this what it's going to be like staying here with you? Are you going to be my therapist?" His voice has dropped, and I can tell he's angry—that and the way he's stabbing at his eggs like they insulted him.

"No, I won't bring it up again. I just had to get it off my chest. I want you to know that if you ever want to talk, I'm here and I'll listen."

James doesn't respond but focuses all his attention on his food, taking another round of bacon. At least he's not running away.

"How long have you been with the team?" James breaks his own silence and awkwardness that has settled in the room.

"A few years. I'm the newest member."

"How did you find them?"

"One of my old commanders was friends with Mika and knew I was struggling to find work, so he hooked me up."

James nods but doesn't ask any other questions. Instead, he focuses on the food in front of him.

"I'll show you to your room when you're done eating."

James nods again. *Note taken.* I guess talking time is over and his walls have gone back up.

James gets up, and before I can take my plate to the kitchen, he grabs it as well as the one in the middle of the table. He takes them all in and drops them into the dishwasher, once again acting as if he knows everything about my home and where everything goes.

He's such an interesting mix of coldness and comfort.

"Can you make it up the stairs?" James asks, coming to stand next to the table.

"Yeah, I'll manage. Do you mind carrying my bag?"

"I got it." He picks up his bag, slinging it over his shoulder before picking mine up as well, making sure not to jostle his broken arm too much.

"How's the arm holding up?"

"Sore." His responses are clipped and he's avoiding my eyes again.

If I could break down those walls right now, I would. I'd do anything to see something other than pain in his eyes.

He goes up the stairs first and I follow behind, taking it slowly and making sure not to put too much weight on my boot.

"Your room is the one right here at the top of the steps." I point from behind him. He steps into the guest bedroom, drops his bag, and turns back to me expectantly.

"Mine's at the end of the hall. You have your own bathroom, but there's also one in the hallway if you need it for some reason."

James follows me to the end of the hall, and I open the door to my room. It's a large suite with a sitting area to the right and a huge ensuite.

"Impressive," he says, stepping into the room and looking at the mini-library I have in my sitting area. He drops the bag in front of my dresser and goes to leave.

"James."

He turns.

"I want to talk with you sometime about what I did at your apartment."

"Let's just pretend it didn't happen."

"Oh, James, I refuse to do that, because I'd love to do it again and again if you're up for it." I step into his space, pinning him against the dresser. Not too aggressively, but I need him to understand that I want him and intend to pursue him.

"Luke, I don't know why you think I'm interested in you. I mean…I'm not even into guys."

I take a step back and look at James closely.

"Is that true, James, or is that another wall that you've built?"

He doesn't respond, but he also doesn't move away from me, either.

"I'll lay this out for you, James. I'm interested in you, curious about you, and want to get to know you better. That's because I like you, James."

James' cheeks blush dark burgundy, but he still doesn't move away from me.

"Like right now, James. You have no idea what you're doing to me, how attractive you are when you blush." I want to lean in, to pin his body to the dresser again, but I don't want to scare him or move too quickly.

I lean in so our faces are just a few inches from each other and look from his eyes to his lips. *Those full fucking lips.* I move ever so slowly, press my lips to his, and wait for him to pull away—except he doesn't.

James stiffens under my lips, but quickly relaxes, leaning into the kiss. I pull back slightly before going in for another kiss. Pressing my lips to his, I open my mouth, inviting him to reciprocate. There's a slight pause before James opens his mouth, meeting me kiss for kiss.

It starts slow before my need becomes too much to handle. I deepen the kiss, pushing James back and pressing our bodies together. I wince as I bump my booted foot against the dresser, but I don't break the kiss. To my surprise, I feel his hand at my waist, gripping me and pulling me closer. James smells faintly of sweat and nature from our run through the woods and tastes ever so slightly like beer.

He's matching my desire, and I can feel the hard length of him pressing into my own as we meld into one another. I'm burning, *dying* to take off this damn hoodie. I pull back from his lips and kiss his sharp jawline, running rushed kisses from his jaw to his ear lobe. I pause to suck and tease it before continuing to kiss down his neck. I'm spurred on by the soft moans leaving James' kiss-swollen lips as he leans his head away, giving me better access to his neck.

I need him naked now, but I stop. I don't want to overwhelm him.

I pull back, resting my head on his shoulder.

"Fuck, James. I can't control myself around you."

James shifts against my weight and turns us. Suddenly, I'm leaning against the dresser and James is leaning into me.

"What are you doing?"

James doesn't say anything, but his gaze drops to the bulge in my pants before he glances back at me, almost as if he's asking permission. I take my hands from his shoulders and slowly unzip my pants, not looking away from him as he watches every movement of my hands. The only sound in the room is our ragged breathing and the sound of my zipper.

James pauses briefly before slowly dropping to his knees so he's kneeling in front of me.

I stop breathing as he deftly finishes undoing my pants and pulls my cock free of my boxer briefs.

Am I dreaming?

Is James actually on his knees, with my cock in his hand, looking at me with those eyes?

James looks up at me and maintains eye contact as he puts the tip of my dick in his mouth. He pulls my length into his mouth, hollowing his cheeks and sucking. I gasp with the feel of him and close my eyes as my head falls back with the exquisite feeling of what James is doing to my dick.

I open my eyes and watch as James sucks and swirls his tongue, try not to thrust too deeply into his throat. His mouth feels so good, all hot and wet around me. I'm managing to control myself until he groans, letting me thrust my full length in until it hits the back of his throat and then just a little further. My legs shake and the aching in my balls becomes almost too much to handle. I run my hands through James' thick, dark hair. He swallows around my length, and I almost come on the spot.

"*Fuck*, James."

He moans again around my dick, humming in pleasure as he picks up speed and works my cock in and out of his mouth. Pulling my dick from his mouth, he keeps eye contact as he licks from my balls, up my shaft, to the tip, licking away the precum. My dick jumps with every lick.

"I'm going to come soon." I don't even recognize the sound of my voice. It's thick and raspy.

"Mmmhmm." James moans around my cock and sucks me deeper. I can feel my release building and know that I won't be able to hold it off much longer. Every muscle in my body tightens as the tension grows.

"James…" I manage to get out as a warning before I cum. James doesn't seem to mind, swallowing my release as I come completely undone against the dresser. I swear my bones are gone as my legs shake. James doesn't stop, gently continuing to suck and lick as I come down from my climax, licking the tip of my cock as he finishes.

I can see how hard he is and want to repay the favor. I reach down for him, pulling him up from his knees and crushing his mouth with a bruising kiss. Tasting myself on his tongue, I deepened the kiss. I pull away, resting my forehead against his.

"Holy shit, that was amazing. Let me…" I reach between us and grab his length through his pants. He shudders against my forehead before leaning his head back, groaning as I undo his pants and stroke down the length of his dick.

God, even his dick is gorgeous.

"You…you don't have to," James sputters as I tighten my grip before letting go.

"Get on the bed," I instruct him. To my pleasure, he obeys.

Good boy.

He sits on the edge of the bed, and I kneel in front of him, starting with removing his shoes, socks, and then his pants and briefs. I then pull his shirt off and am left breathless as I take in his body.

"You are gorgeous, James." He's reclined on his elbows, his abs popping as he flexes, and his pec muscles working overtime to keep him elevated. His skin is olive-painted with white and darker brown patches from his scars.

I can't stop looking at his body as I climb on top of him, leaning down to kiss him again, this time slower. I want to take my time and take in his body. I push him back so he's lying down. I'm overcome with pleasure when his hand finds its way to the small of my back, where he presses to ease me down on top of him more.

I kiss his jawline again, then down his neck to his collarbone. I kiss along the right one, then the left, before snagging one of his pebbled nipples in my mouth. I nip it lightly and revel in the sound he makes as he grinds his hard dick into my abdomen, making it slick with his precum. I want to fuck him so badly, but tonight is not the night for that.

Tonight, I want to enjoy his body and the sounds he makes as he cums.

I continue kissing down his body, taking in every tightening muscle that I leave behind, and pause as I come to his hard cock.

I want to go slow; I want to taste every inch of him. But my need to make him cum makes me desperate.

I start at his balls, sucking one then the other, and then lick my way up the length of his cock. I swirl my tongue around the tip of his dick before taking his length into my mouth. I can barely manage it before I have to pull back. He is perfect in every way.

James' hand tangles in my hair as he takes a handful, guiding my rhythm as I suck and lick. I feel him get impossibly harder as we find the rhythm that works for him.

"Oh God, Luke. That feels so good."

"You want me to keep going? Tell me what you want, James."

"Just like that, fuck." James' hips buck as I take him deeper than before, letting him drive into my throat. He holds me before letting me go so I can catch my breath.

James guides my head as he continues to thrust into my mouth.

I feel his entire body tighten and know that he's close. He bucks, groaning with his release. I take all of him, feeling his cum hit the back of my throat as I swallow it down.

I'm completely undone.

CHAPTER 9

James

As I return to my body, I'm immediately hit with the guilt and shame of what we just did. What *I* just did. I can't believe I did that, with Luke no less. I don't know what came over me. Seeing him there in front of me, telling me how much he wanted me, fucked with my head.

I'm still lying halfway on the bed, completely naked, with Luke flopped next to me on his stomach. I cover my face with my arm cast and contemplate what to do next.

"Don't overthink it, James." Luke's voice is quiet, and he sounds tired.

I turn my head, lifting my arm to look at the man lying next to me. Luke is stunning. Every time he looks at me, I struggle to control myself.

"How do you know I'm overthinking it?"

"I can see your wheels spinning."

"What did we just do, Luke?" I can't look away from him or his swollen lips.

"What we wanted to do, James. I wanted you and you wanted me. We're both adults. There's nothing to feel guilty about."

"We work together and barely know each other," I continue, trying to make him understand.

"Then let me get to know you, James. Open up to me, let me in." Luke has risen to his elbows and looks down at me as I lay beside him. He takes a hand and places it on my bare chest.

"I want to get to know you, James. I don't see you as a quick fuck or someone to just have some fun with. I like what we just did, and I want to do it again. I want to do more with you than just suck your cock."

I turn my head away from him, embarrassment flooding me.

"Look at me." Luke's calloused hand moves from my chest to my chin.

"I want you to be mine, James. I want all of you. I would love it if you wanted to be with me, too. But I agree—I don't know you and you don't know me that well, either. So why don't we get to know each other and then we can see where we can take this?"

I wouldn't have expected Luke to be like this. He comes off as flippant and immature, yet here he is, telling me exactly what I need to hear.

I shake off that thought. "I don't know if I can do that, Luke. I don't know if I have the ability, the capacity, to open up and care for someone else." I sit up, push Luke's hand off my chest, and stand, grabbing my pants in the process.

Luke follows, sitting up and pulling on his boxer briefs before sitting back down on the edge of the bed. I can feel his eyes following every move I make as I gather my clothes and put them on.

"Are you willing to try it, though?" Luke asks softly.

I have my back turned to him as I pull my shirt. I don't hear him move, but suddenly his hand is on my shoulder, turning me to face him.

"What about it, James? Will you give it a go with me?" His blue eyes search mine as I take in this man standing before me.

"I…need to think about it. I'm not sure about any of this, Luke. People don't know that I'm gay. *Kee* doesn't even know."

"I get it, it's scary. I don't know the whole story about what happened between you and Shawn, but I know there's more to it. I don't want you overthinking everything. Don't compare this to what you've experienced in the past. Can you try to do that?" Luke holds onto my shoulder and gives it a soft squeeze before letting go.

"Luke, wait. I…I want to tell you about everything. Shit, I haven't talked to anyone about it in years, but I need you to be patient with me. It might take me a while to find my voice again."

I'm looking at his back, ready for him to tell me to forget about it and that it sounds like it will be too much work. But to my surprise, he turns around, takes two steps towards me, and kisses me.

It happens so quickly I don't even have time to register what's happening before he pulls back, cupping my face. "I'll wait for as long as you need, James."

I nod and close my eyes as Luke leans in, his soft, plush lips caressing mine gently before he deepens the kiss, making my heartbeat speed up and my thoughts race.

He pulls away again and I find myself leaning towards him for more. He gladly obliges me with another kiss.

"You should go get some rest before I do all the things I want to do with you," Luke breathes.

I can't help but smile at his remark. I glance down, looking at the bulge in his boxers, and want to suck his dick all over again.

There's something about Luke that turns me on. It's the first time in a long time that I've felt this way.

"Right, bed." I manage to walk out the door before I decide to go for another round with him.

"Good night, James," Luke calls from behind me. I don't even have to turn around to know that he's got his signature smirk on his face.

I raise my hand in acknowledgment and head down the hall to my room where my bag is still sitting just past the threshold.

Walking into the room, I flip on the switch and take in the homey atmosphere as I shut the door behind me, leaning against it. My thoughts are racing now that I'm alone and away from Luke's polarizing energy.

I must be out of my mind. That's it, it's the concussion.

I step into the shower's hot water and let it run down my sore body. I've got new bruises and cuts after today and the hot water feels great as it eases my tired muscles and joints. Closing my eyes, I lean into the water and try not to think about anything.

If only it were that easy.

I can feel Luke's hands on my body, see him, smell him, taste him, even as I wash him from my body. I can't help but replay the moments from his bedroom in my mind as I shower, lingering on the way his lips felt against mine, the way he moans when he cums.

Fuck. If I keep thinking about it, I'll get hard again and will have to take care of myself this time.

Shaking my head, I step out of the shower and towel off. Walking naked through the room, I grab my bag and pull out some gray sweatpants to sleep in.

Lying in bed, my mind drifts in another direction. *Do I tell Luke the truth about Shawn? Do I tell him that we were partners for five years as well as teammates before he was killed? How his death almost destroyed me and that it took me years to piece myself back together again?*

Rolling to my side, I try to settle my mind so that I can get some rest. I take a deep breath in and another out. The tightening in my chest grows, but the breath work helps to loosen it. The events from today finally catch up to me as I feel the heaviness of sleep in the back of my eyes.

There's blood everywhere I look. It's all over my hands, on my shirt, pants, and shoes. I can't wipe it off. The ground is covered in it. A few feet away is a body, twisted inhumanly as it lay broken on the asphalt. All I can hear is my breathing echoing in my ears. I take a step towards the body, then another. My legs feel like they weigh a hundred pounds. It takes everything I have to keep moving forward.

Please, don't let this happen again. Please.

I draw closer to the broken form and feel my breath stuttering in my chest. I can't breathe, I can't think. The darkness on the edge of my vision grows, but not before I see the face of the person lying in front of me.

Shawn.

His blank eyes stare up at me from his grotesquely turned head. Everything is wrong. This shouldn't have happened. We weren't even supposed to be on that mission. We were both supposed to be on leave. On vacation, just the two of us.

No, no, no, not again.

I crumble next to Shawn's shattered and bloodied body as a scream rips free from my raw throat.

"James! James!"

Shaking. My body is *shaking* as I fall apart, screaming Shawn's name.

"James! Wake up!"

The shaking continues and suddenly, I'm ripped away from Shawn.

I shoot up in bed, almost knocking heads with Luke who is leaning over and shaking me.

I shuffle backward until my hot back is against the cool headboard. I put my head between my knees, trying to catch my breath.

"James, talk to me. Are you okay?" Luke's voice is soft and soothing as he places a hand on my shoulder.

"Just a bad dream," I manage between pants.

"It sounded like more than just a bad dream. You were screaming, James. I've never heard someone scream like that before."

"I'm sorry."

"Don't be sorry. I want to make sure that you're okay. You scared the shit outta me."

"I'm sorry." It's the only thing I can think of to say.

"You're fucking sheets are soaked through with sweat." Luke continues running a hand down my back.

It's oddly comforting. His touch serves as an anchor, letting me know that this is real and that I'm not still stuck in a dream.

My breathing settles and I stretch my legs out in front of me, leaning my head back against the headboard. My eyes are still closed, but I can feel Luke's stare.

"Come to bed with me," he says, his hand now resting on my upper arm.

"Not in the mood for that, Luke."

"Not for sex! *Jesus,* I'm not a complete animal. I was thinking it might be good to have someone sleep with you and keep you company. Might help with the bad dreams."

I look at Luke for the first time since he woke me from my nightmare. His long hair is everywhere, completely disheveled. His blue eyes are soft in the low, dim light of the bedside lamp. He's in a pair of cotton shorts and that's it.

"Come on, James. It can't hurt anything, and I won't try anything funny. Come to bed with me?" He raises his golden eyebrows and all I can do is nod in agreement.

He helps me untangle from the sheets and we walk down the hall to his room together.

I'm still lost in the dream. Images of Luke and Shawn mingling in my mind as I follow them both down the hallway. It's hard to stay focused on what's real.

Luke shuts the door behind me. I shuffle over to the bed and sit on the edge. Luke climbs into bed from the other side. I feel it sink as he lays down.

"James?"

I turn and look at Luke. There's no pressure in his eyes, just concern. I swing my legs over and slide under the blankets, immediately feeling the warmth of his body. I'm tense at first, but it doesn't take long for my body to settle and for sleep to start tugging at my mind again. I can't quite let it take me all the way under just yet. I roll to my side and sigh as my mind tumbles back to the nightmare.

I feel the mattress move and suddenly, Luke's arm slides around my waist. He pulls me tightly against his warm, hard body.

"Luke, I thought you said no sex?"

"I did, and I meant it. I want you to feel safe and to relax so that you can get a good night's rest. Can you do that for me?"

I nod into the pillow and concentrate on the feel of Luke's arm around my waist, the way his body feels against mine.

It doesn't take long for my exhausted mind and body to give in, sleep tugging me under yet again.

Consciousness comes fluttering back to me and the first thing I realize is that I'm insanely comfortable. The second thing is that the space behind me is cold, and Luke is gone. There's warmth drifting through the room from the bathroom where I can hear the shower running.

I sit up slowly in the bed, pushing myself up so that I'm resting against the headrest. I take a moment to reflect on what happened last night. It's hard for me to understand why Luke would want someone like me.

I look toward the shut door and, for a moment, entertain the idea of going in there and showering with him. Just the thought of it makes me hard.

What would he do if I joined him?

I don't know if it's the fact that I slept so well once I was in his bed or the way he treats me and the patience he's shown, but I'm feeling bold and confident this morning.

I haven't felt like this since Shawn and I first started dating. It's refreshing and sad at the same time. I long for what I once had and feel nervous about what could possibly happen with Luke.

I swing my legs out of the bed and walk over to the bathroom door, leaning my forehead against it as I contemplate what to do.

I pull back my hand and knock softly.

"Yeah?" Luke sounds worried, which is understandable given everything that transpired the night before.

"Can I join you?" I hate how tentative I sound, how obvious it is that I'm scared.

"Join me? *Hell yeah*," Luke calls back. I'm pushing the door open before I can stop myself.

I'm greeted by the warm mist from the shower, and I notice the size of the bathroom. It's massive, with a huge shower in one corner and a large jacuzzi tub in the other. Luke is in the shower where I can see the shadow of his body through the fogged-up glass.

I'm taking my sweats off and moving toward the shower as soon as I see him. Thank God we were given waterproof casts.

I open the door of the shower slowly and step into the warmth. Luke's already turned around to greet me, my eyes roaming over his wet body as it glistens from the water.

Damn, he is beautiful.

Luke smiles at me and reaches for my hand, pulling me closer to him and the warm water.

"Did you sleep well?" he asks, moving to the side so I can stand under the shower's spray.

"It was the best I've slept in a long time." I can't take my eyes off him.

"Good." He gives me a soft smile. He's all soft this morning while his body is hard—such a contradiction.

I turn my back to him in the hopes of hiding my raging hard-on. Everything about Luke turns me on and it's damn near impossible to keep myself under control.

Luke's hands find their way to my shoulders as he starts to

lather my body with soap. He starts on my back, then reaches around to my chest before working lower to my abdomen, and then lower still.

Using the suds from the soap, he grips me tightly in his hands and strokes. I shudder with the feel of his hands on my hard cock and lean back into his solid body, letting him support me. My mind clears until the only thing I feel is Luke against my back and his hand increasing both pressure and speed.

"Luke..." It's a broken prayer that leaves my lips as my dick jumps in his hands.

"That's right, I want you to cum for me, James. Let go. Let me bring you pleasure. I want to make you feel good."

The only thing I can say is his name as I lose control.

I sag back into his body and feel his arousal against my ass. I press into it and continue to enjoy the feel of his hands as he runs them up my abdomen and down again.

I'm at a loss for words as I let Luke continue to support and comfort me while I come down.

"We should get out soon or we'll run out of hot water. Why don't you finish cleaning up and meet me downstairs for breakfast?" His whisper against my ear gives me chills. I turn, catching his lips before he can pull away.

"None of that, or I'll have you back in bed and we won't get anything done today," Luke says as the kiss ends.

Luke gives me a quick kiss and steps out of the shower, leaving me to finish washing. It all feels strangely domestic: sleeping, showering, eating together.

"Hey, James!" Luke calls from his room, breaking me from my thoughts.

"Yeah?"

"Stop overthinking and just enjoy it." I can hear the smile in his voice and know that he's laughing at me, but in a good-natured way.

"I'll do my best," I mutter under my breath, ducking my head into the shower spray and trying to simply enjoy the feeling of the water running down my body.

I think I'm enjoying this connection with Luke. But it's been so long that I'm unsure of what is happening here. All the feelings swirling in my head make me more confused than anything else.

By the time I pull myself from my thoughts, the water has started to cool, and the smell of bacon and eggs has permeated the bathroom fog. I quickly dry off and head down the hall to my room to get dressed. After a few minutes of putting on jeans and a sweater, I head downstairs to the kitchen.

Luke doesn't hear me coming, or if he does, he doesn't react, giving me a few seconds to watch him in the kitchen. He's in a pair of well-fitting jeans that hug his muscular thighs and ass, a long-sleeved shirt, and socks. His long, blonde hair is untied and falls around his shoulders, swaying with his movement as he cooks, his broad shoulders flexing with each motion.

Again, I'm reminded of how domestic all of this is. Shawn and I only had a few of these moments when we were together. We spent most of our relationship deployed and surrounded by our team, rarely having times like this one. When we did, we always made sure to take full advantage of staying home, relaxing, enjoying each other's presence without expectation, and cherishing the domestic moments.

"Smells good," I say from the doorway of the kitchen.

Luke turns, giving me a brilliant smile. "Are you hungry?"

"Famished."

"Take a seat, it'll be ready in a minute."

I've barely sat down before Luke is there, serving me a plate full of bacon, eggs, pancakes, and a few sausages. He also brings a glass of water and a cup of coffee.

I wait for him to sit before I dig in. I *am* famished and breakfast has never tasted so good. I rarely cook for myself, so this is a nice change. Shawn always cooked for me.

"Hitting the spot?" Luke asks, watching me from across the table with raised eyebrows.

"Definitely, I was hungrier than I thought. What's on the schedule for today?" I ask, sitting back and chewing on the slightly burnt bacon on my plate.

"We've got a team meeting in about an hour at the main building to discuss our plan for dealing with Dimitri. I'm sure Mika will have assignments for us after the meeting."

"Do you think Dimitri will make a move on the compound?"

"I think he's unhinged enough that he'll try it."

"What are our chances of finding him before he can?"

"He seems exceptionally good at hiding, which is wild considering he's building a small army. I can't believe that the Marshals or DEA haven't been able to find him yet." Luke takes another bite of his pancake and looks at his plate thoughtfully.

"How are you feeling? About everything?" he asks, searching my face as I think about my response.

"About Dimitri or about whatever is going on between us?" I counter, returning his gaze.

"Us," he responds immediately.

"Honestly, I'm not sure how I feel just yet. It's fast, new, and all a bit confusing. I'm trying not to overthink it, but that's hard for me." I return to my food and wait for Luke to respond.

"If there's anything I can do to help you feel more comfortable or less flighty, please tell me. I know I've said this before, but I like you, James. I'd like to see where this goes."

I exhale a breath I didn't know I was holding, realizing that I was waiting for him to tell me to suck it up. As if I don't already know that I need to stop overthinking everything, but that isn't how anxiety works? I can't just turn it off when it gets too much.

"I appreciate that." I look back up and find Luke studying me.

"I'm fine, I promise. If I feel myself spinning out, I'll let you know."

"Not to push or pry, but I'd like to take you to meet Dr. Hardigan, the therapist that we keep on retainer here."

"Do you see her?"

"Yeah, she's helped me deal with the loss of my own team. I still struggle a lot with it, but I have the tools I need to manage my PTSD. It doesn't just go away, but it has gotten easier to deal with."

"I…will think about it. I've done therapy before and it helped for a while, but lately, with everything going on, it's been harder to manage."

Luke nods, his expression gentle and eyes soft as I talk.

"I'm here for you. If you need anything in the meantime, just let me know. I know it's different for everyone and our experiences are our own, but I care and can listen."

I look down at my now empty plate. I would normally turn off my emotions at this point and retreat, but Luke makes me want to share and explore things again.

"Thank you, Luke."

"Anytime, James." He smiles and reaches across the table, dishing me up another serving of crispy bacon and eggs.

"Eat up. It's going to be a long-ass day."

CHAPTER 10

Luke

James eats everything I put in front of him, making me feel like I know what I'm doing in the kitchen. I haven't fed another person in a long time, but I'm finding that I like to see him eating.

I watch as he finishes his second plate and gathers our plates.

"I'll clean up," James offers, standing and grabbing the plates before I can protest.

I follow behind with the dishes from the food and drop them next to the sink for James. Thank God they gave him a waterproof cast too; it's making things a lot easier for him. I look down at my booted foot and wince. I wish I had my crutches. Still putting all my weight on my leg sucks, especially when I have to be on my feet for a while or do a lot of walking.

I sit back at the table, sipping my coffee as James works in the kitchen. It doesn't escape me that he is in my kitchen, doing dishes. It should feel weird, but it doesn't. It feels right. *He feels right.* James does quick work of the dishes, then comes back out to the dining room and stands next to the table.

"Ready to head out?" he asks.

I check my watch. "Yup, we should get going so we're not late." I get up and walk towards the front door, slipping on my one boot and grabbing the keys to my truck. Normally, I would walk, but seeing how I've got a bum foot, driving is the next best thing.

"Do you need to grab anything before we go?" I ask James who's standing behind me, watching me struggle with putting my boot on. He's got the smallest smile on his lips as he watches.

"Enjoying the show?" I ask. James' smile grows and he chuckles.

"Do you need help getting your shoe on?"

"A little late, James. I've already got it on," I kid back.

"Come on, let's get going." He chuckles and opens the front door. The cold morning air blasts both of us in the face. I reach over quickly to grab a coat and pass James my extra one before we step out into the brisk air.

The snow crunches under our feet and I notice that James stays at my side, ready to help me if I slip or my foot gets too painful.

"Wanna drive?" I ask, handing him the keys.

"Sure." Taking the keys from me, he walks me to the passenger-side door and opens it for me before shutting it and walking around the truck to the driver's side.

"We should've started the truck earlier so it could warm up," James notes as we both huddle in the cold cab, waiting for the heat to start working. It takes a few minutes for the heat to start blasting as James gets us rolling towards the main building.

Parking a few minutes later, we walk into the war room to find that we are the last ones to arrive. Everyone is already sitting around the table and all turn to look at us as we walk in.

"Well, look who decided to show up, just barely on time as usual," Mika ribs as James and I walk in and take our seats toward the end of the table.

I catch Kee giving James a look and him nodding back to her before I turn my attention back to Mika.

"I wouldn't dream of being late to this one," I respond with a grin. Mika and the rest of the team smile in return as Mika shakes his head at me. It's nice to have a team lead who can joke and make things lighter. Our work can be dark and stressful, so having a sense of humor goes a long way.

"Alright, now that everyone's here, let's get started," Mika begins. "We've been monitoring Dimitri's movements. He's good at flying under the radar, having a lot of places and people in town that are willing to hide him. We know he's gathered his men and there's been activity at the docks."

Mika pauses, looking at each of us before he continues, "That being said, we're expecting him to make a move in the next couple of days. We can assume that he knows where the compound is after yesterday's run-in, so it will only be a matter of time before he attacks. I want us to be ready for that. John, walk us through our defenses and strategy."

John, a man in his late forties who's built like a freight train, stands up. "Right. So, we've doubled our patrols along the fence line and are monitoring the cameras 24/7. We've noted a few random cars that have done drive-bys both yesterday and early this morning. It's safe to say that those are some of Dimitri's men. Everyone take a radio and have it turned to channel three."

John looks around the room and is met by a series of nods from everyone. I notice Hannah taking Gray's hand, and Marcus looking at Kee before everyone turns their attention back to John.

I fight the urge to look at James as his knee brushes mine under the table, settling for putting my hand on his thigh.

He straightens before relaxing, leaning towards me in his chair.

"We will equip everyone with protective gear and arm those who will be helping us defend the compound." John looks directly at Hannah. "Doctor Winters, I'm assuming you'll be hanging back in the medical center with Finn if anything goes down?"

Hannah nods affirmatively, still clutching Gray's hand on top of the table. "Yes. Neko, will you be there as well?"

"No, I'll be out with the team just in case someone needs medical attention in the field."

"What about James and Luke? They're both injured," Kee mentions while looking towards us.

James shifts away from me before answering, "I can still use a firearm with my one good hand," he grumbles, shooting Kee a look that has even me squirming in my seat.

"I'd like to be on the frontline with the team if possible. I can set up and provide as much coverage as possible so that I don't have to move as much," I offer.

"I'd like you to be out there with us as well, Luke," Mika confirms. "When the time comes, we'll set you up in a location that will help us defend the compound."

"Thanks, Mika." I give him an appreciative nod and squeeze James' leg as it begins to bounce.

I want to tell him not to be anxious and that everything will be fine. But there are too many people in the room and I don't want to lie to him. If there were ever a time to be nervous, it's now.

I'm also not one to placate and give empty reassurances. I don't know if everything will be fine. There's a good chance we'll be outmanned and outgunned when we take on Dimitri. All I can do is provide James with support and be as solid as I can for him.

John sits back down and Mika continues, "We're going to get everyone's gear together now; take it with you to your bunks. We will reach out on the radio if we need anything from you. You're also all staying with members of the team. They know this place well. I recommend taking a tour of the grounds so that you have a better idea of what we're defending. Any questions?"

He glances around the table and is met with shaking heads. "Alright, let's get you folks geared up then."

Everyone disperses. James and I are the last ones out of the room, right behind Mika.

I reach over and link my pinky with his, giving it a squeeze before letting go. James doesn't react outwardly, but I see the deep burgundy returning to his cheeks and smile. As I look away, I catch Kee's eyes. She's staring right at me, looking shocked. I quickly glance at James and am relieved that he hasn't noticed what she saw.

Kee motions for me to come over to her, and I oblige, unsure if I'm in for a scolding or a congratulations.

"Well, well, so you finally made a move?" Kee whispers as I walk up to her.

"I'm taking it slow; I promise." I look back at James, who is completely engrossed in the gear Mika and John are laying out.

"Good, I think that's what he needs. I'm a little worried he's going to be distracted going into this, and we need everyone to be focused right now. I want to make sure that you're keeping that in mind as well as James' wellbeing."

"I have feelings for James and I think he has feelings for me,

too. We're exploring and seeing if there's something there. But I understand what you're saying and I can assure you that we're both very focused on the mission."

"Listen, I care about James. He's my partner, I need him to be okay. The last thing I want is for him to have his mind and his emotions messed with."

"I understand. I'm not trying to do that, I swear. We're taking things slow, and if James thinks it's too much at any point, all he has to do is tell me and I'll back off."

I continue, "I know that James is important to you. He's important to me, too. I want nothing but the best for him."

Kee looks me over again and finally nods. "Fine, but if you hurt him, I will come for you. I will make your life a living hell, Luke, and that's a promise." Kee flashes a smile and gives me a soft punch to the arm, letting me know she's joking but also very serious about her threat.

I smile as she finishes threatening me. "It's good that James has someone like you in his corner, Kee."

I grasp her shoulder, giving it a squeeze as James and Marcus join the two of us.

"Everything good here?" Marcus asks, looking between Kee and me.

"Yup, everything's all good," I respond. "Let's get you geared up," I say, almost reaching for James' hand, forgetting where we are. I don't care if people see, but I'm not sure if James is ready for people to know.

James looks from Kee and back to me before following the motion of my hand back towards the gear.

"Hey, James! Come find me later. I wanna chat," Kee calls after us.

"Will do," James responds as we walk up to where the body armor is.

"What was that all about?" he asks.

"You saw that?"

"Yeah."

I pause, biting my lower lip and get a small sense of pleasure as I see James' eyes track the movement. "She…wanted to make sure that I have good intentions towards you."

His eyes snap up from my lips to my eyes, darting between them as if he can tell if I'm joking from my eyes.

"She *knows?*" he whispers-shouts. I see a small bit of panic working its way into his eyes.

"She saw me grab your pinky." My stomach drops at his reaction, my chest tightens seeing the panic in his eyes. I'm overcome with guilt.

"Shit."

"James, it's okay. She doesn't care that it's you and me. She wants to make sure that *you're* okay emotionally."

"This is a bad idea." James turns and walks out of the armory before I can react.

I hobble after him. "James! James!" I manage to catch the driver's side door before he can shut it.

"I can't do this. I can't do this again," he repeats over and over. The panic has grown to a full-blown, wild-eyed look.

"James, take a breath. This doesn't mean anything. Everything is fine. Kee knew I was pursuing you before this. I talked to her when we were on our way to Russia. She doesn't care and she's not going to tell anyone."

"It's not that, Luke. It's the team. I can't go through having the team look at us like we're a liability, like we're weaker than them because we're gay, because we're together. I can't do that again. I can't have them look at me differently because of it. This was a bad idea."

He's rambling as the panic takes hold of himYet all I can think to do is to kiss him.

I grab his face in my hands and slam my lips into his, cutting off his rambling.

It surprises him enough that he stops talking and inhales sharply. I pull away, but don't let go of his face.

"James. The team knows that I'm gay and they don't care. We're a team and we have each other's backs. They accept me for who I am and will accept you as well. Fuck, they'll be happy for us."

His breathing has steadied a bit, but his eyes are still wild as he looks around, worry creasing his forehead.

"James, trust me. You have nothing to worry about here. Whatever happened with your old team, with Shawn, it's not going to happen here."

"You don't know that, Luke. You don't know how people will react. I thought my old team would be fine, but when they found out, everything changed. They treated us so differently, and then when we moved in together, they all but kicked us off the team. I thought they were my friends, my brothers. And all of that went out the window in a matter of seconds once they found out." James' breathing hitches, the panic is back.

"Breathe, James. Please just breathe. I can assure you that this team is different. There are already couples on this team. It's not my place to say who, but everyone is on board with it. They support it." I lean in and rest my forehead against his, whispering a kiss across his lips to calm him.

"Luke, I don't know if I can do this. I'm freaking out." James' rough, deep voice is strained.

"Let's get you back to the house to talk more." I slide in as James moves into the passenger seat.

"What about the gear?" he asks as I start the truck down the road, back to my house.

"I'll swing back by and grab it a little later. I want to get you home."

"I'm sorry, I'm a fucking mess." I glance over at James. He's bent over, resting his elbows on his knees and holding his head up with his hands. I can see his back heaving with every strained breath.

"You don't need to apologize, James. Never apologize for what you can't control."

We ride the rest of the way in silence and soon pull up to the house.

"Let's get inside and get warm." James is already out and walking to the house before I'm barely out of the truck.

He's running.

If I wasn't in a boot, I would be able to catch him. But as it is, he's already halfway into the house before I reach him.

"James …" I grab his arm and hang on as he tries to pull away. I push us both into the house and shut the door behind me, pushing James against it.

"Stop fighting me, please," I whisper, holding onto him from behind as he leans his head against the cool door.

After a minute, he says, "Please let me go. I'm calm." I slowly let go and he turns in my arms, leaning his back against the door.

"I'm fine," he whispers as he tilts his head back, resting it on the door. His eyes are closed, his full, dark eyelashes kiss the tops

of his high olive cheekbones, which are brushed wine-red. His lips are chapped from the cold and I fight everything in my body not to kiss them again.

"You're not, though, James," I whisper back, waiting for him to insist otherwise.

Instead, a shudder runs through his body and he slides down the door until he's pooled on the floor. He has his knees up to his chest, arms around his knees, and head buried between them.

I sit on the floor beside him, pulling him sideways until his body rests against mine. James' shoulders shake as he cries silently. After several minutes, he unfurls, wrapping his arms around my neck and burying his face into the space where my neck and collarbone meet. I pull him into a tight hug and let him cry until he's gone completely still.

"You're right. I'm not fine. I need help, but I'm scared to delve into my past again. Into the trauma of what happened with Shawn, all of it. I don't know if I'll survive it again." His warm breath whispers across my neck, tickling it as he shares his fears.

"You're not alone this time, James. You have me, Kee, and the rest of the team as well. We're all here for you. You've gotta let us in a bit." I tighten my hold on him, pulling him in closer. I want him as close as possible, as if it would allow him to feel just how much he means to me, to all of us.

"We can have some coffee or tea, start a fire, and sit on the couch to relax. How does that sound?"

"That would be better than the floor."

"James! Did you just tell a joke?" I pull back to look at him, feigning disbelief.

"Fuck you, Luke." He lets go of my neck and gets up, making his way to the living room as I get up and go to the kitchen.

"Coffee or tea?" I call out.

"Coffee, please." His voice is still raspy and full of raw emotion, but he seems to be in control of himself again.

"On it. Why don't you start a fire?"

"Will do."

I hear him bustling about as I start a pot of coffee and pull out a pizza from the freezer. It's not glamorous, but it'll feed us in a bind. Right now, I don't have the mental capacity to fix a full meal.

I peek out of the kitchen and watch as James throws several logs into the fireplace along with some kindling. He's got a fire going in a matter of a few minutes and has settled on the leather couch. He looks a little shell-shocked, which is understandable, as he's likely coming down from the adrenaline and rush of the panic attack.

It'll be good to get him a bit of food. The caffeine is probably not as good for him, but I don't want to police him too much.

The smell of pizza and coffee, a weird mix, starts to fill the kitchen. But as I walk toward the living room, all I can smell is the wood burning in the fireplace. I sit next to James and pass him a cup of coffee. He takes it black, which is strange to me, as I've got to have creamer and a bit of sugar to get through my cup. Coffee isn't my favorite, but it fuels me, so I make do with it.

"Are you feeling any better?"

"Do you ever get tired of asking that?" He looks down at his coffee mug as if he could read his future in its endless blackness.

"No. I ask because I care."

"How did you end up like this? So...open?"

I chuckle and look at my tan coffee. "Well, I got really lucky. I have amazing parents. They're both teachers and very thoughtful. They also couldn't care less that I'm gay. They did have a problem

with me going into the military and they do have a problem with the line of work I'm in, but they love me. They've been there for me through everything. They let me live with them for a few years after I got out of the service until I got back on my feet and fixed up the farmhouse that I live in now. What about your parents?"

James looks up at the fire, scoffing. "Pretty much the opposite of yours, it sounds like. My dad was former military and a total hardass. I tried to hide what I was from them until I got out of high school, but they found out when they found me and one of my guy friends together. I thought they were out of town for the weekend, but they came home early because my mom got sick. Needless to say, it didn't go over well. I thought my dad was going to beat the shit out of me, and he did."

"Damn, James, I'm sorry." I reach for his leg and rest my hand lightly on his thigh above his knee. It's become a habit when I want to comfort him, but he seems to be okay with it.

"It was completely normal to me. I didn't know that wasn't how other parents were. I thought everyone's parents were like mine: hard, cold, and just fucking mean. I went into the military as soon as I graduated from high school, partially to get away from them, but also because it was expected of me."

"What happened when they found out about Shawn?"

"They never did. I only spoke to them a few times after I left, and we hadn't spoken in years by the time that Shawn and I were together. They never knew about him or what happened to him."

Nothing I can say could make any of this better, so I squeeze James' leg in the hopes of comforting him.

"I didn't have anywhere to go when I got out of the military. My partner had just died, and I couldn't bring myself to go back to our home. I couldn't walk through that place, so full of life and memories. Everything reminded me of him, so I hired a company to clear it out and sell the place. I never went back. I moved here and started with the firm almost immediately."

"Damn, you didn't take time off or anything to grieve?"

"No, I didn't want to stop or to think about it. I didn't want it to be real, so I pushed it all aside. Compartmentalized. That's what they teach us in the military, right? I was doing okay until I was on a job where one of the primaries was killed and it sent me into a tailspin. The firm sent me off to therapy and it took *months* for me to process it all fully and to learn to manage the PTSD. Obviously, it's serving me well. I left that firm shortly after and started working with Kee after that."

James looks down at his cup of coffee again, sniffling softly. "I miss him every fucking day and there isn't a single thing I can do to make that go away." His confession is a broken whisper. I immediately pull him into my body, as if I can take his pain away just from touching him.

I cup the back of his neck and draw him in, letting him collapse into me as sobs wrack his body again.

"It's okay, James. I've got you." I hold tightly onto him, anchoring him to me and this place, to this moment.

We sit like this for at least ten minutes, neither of us moving until the sound of the timer on the oven goes off. The smell of pizza blends with the wood from the fireplace.

"I've gotta get up and grab that. I'll be right back," I whisper, lightly brushing my lips across James' forehead as I get up. He nods and leans away, untangling himself from me.

I walk to the kitchen, turn the timer off, and grab the pizza from the oven. Cutting it, I split it between two plates and return to the living room, passing the hot pizza to James.

"Sorry, it's not much, but I didn't want to spend time cooking. I want to be here for you."

"Thank you for being so understanding. I've been closed off from everyone for so long. It's like I'm rediscovering who I am."

"Anytime. I'm more than just good looks, ya know." James graces me with a full smile at my poor joke. We settle into silence to eat and sip the rest of our coffee.

I finish my pizza and get up. "I'm going back up to the armory to grab our gear. Why don't you hang out here and get some rest? It won't take me long."

"You don't need me to come along?" he asks, handing me his empty plate.

"Nope, I got your gear for Russia, so I know your sizes and everything. I've got it covered. Help yourself to anything in the house." After placing the dishes in the sink, I grab my coat and limp out the front door, only to run into Kee about to knock on the door.

"Hey, Kee."

"Hey, I wanted to check in with James. We haven't been able to talk much since yesterday."

"Sounds good, um, just maybe take it easy on him. He's having a bit of a rough day. He's okay, just a bit raw."

Kee nods and walks past me into the house.

Hopping into my truck, I head back to the armory and start loading up gear. It looks like someone has already set mine aside, so it's quick work to gather what James needs. I'm almost done when Neko saunters in.

"Hey, Neko. How's Finn doing?"

"He's doing well. You should stop in, he hasn't seen you in a bit." Neko claps me on the back with a huge grin on his face.

"Yeah, I feel like shit about that. I'll swing through on my way back to the house."

"How's James?" Neko gives me a knowing smile again. He's got us figured out.

"I think he has a long road ahead of him, but he'll get there. He's dealing with a lot right now. Emotions that he's been pushing down are coming back up. The explosion really rattled him."

"If we need to pull in Doc, let me know. I'll give her a call."

"Thanks, Neko."

Clapping Neko on the shoulder, I walk back to the truck, tossing our equipment into the passenger seat. I've just sat in the driver's seat when something flashes across my vision and the world outside the pickup explodes.

CHAPTER 11

James

One minute, Luke is leaving and the next, Kee is walking in. I brace myself for what's about to come. I don't know how she will handle the news about Luke and me. My entire body tenses with the anticipation of her being revolted by it.

"Wow, Luke's place is not what I expected." Kee looks around, taking in the rustic, minimal feel of the place.

"I was expecting a full bachelor pad with a pool table and maybe a pinball machine or something. Definitely not this." She walks over and sits in the leather chair perpendicular to the couch.

"How is it, staying here with Luke?" She's starting slowly, but I can see the questions swirling behind her eyes.

"It's going well. Luke…is not what I expected." I pause, then decide to get it over with. "I think…he might become someone special to me." I study her face, looking for disgust or anger, but I see only surprise.

"In what way, James?" Kee is going to make me spell it out, but that's fair. I need to say it, I need to say the words out loud for myself and Luke.

"I think I'm interested in Luke. Romantically." I pause again, searching her eyes.

Kee's face is blank for a few seconds before a huge smile breaks free.

"Yes! I knew he had a thing for you!" She gives a little fist pump as if she's just won a game. "I never thought you'd go for him, though. He is literally your opposite in every way."

"You're not angry or anything?"

"*Angry?* Why the hell would I be angry, James? I've been hoping you would find someone since we became partners. This is amazing! I'm frickin' pumped for you."

Kee gets up and before I can protest, she's wrapped me in a hug, squeezing the life out of me.

"You know you can talk to me about anything, right? I'm here for you as a friend and as your partner." The words are whispered into my shoulder as she continues to hug me.

"I know, I'll be better at letting you in. I've been cutting myself off from people for so long that I've forgotten what it's like to have people around me that care."

Kee pulls away. "Okay, I'll leave you alone. But know that if Luke messes up and you need me to take care of him, all you have to do is give me the signal."

I smile and get up to follow her to the door. "How are things with Marcus? Is he recovering well?"

"Yeah, I think he will need some therapy to deal with the trauma from Kiera's torture, but his face is healing well, and the stitches will be able to come out next week."

We're at the door and I pull it open, walking with Kee out the door. As we stand on the front porch, a familiar sound suddenly fills the air.

"*Shit*, that was an explosion!" Kee's surprised cry mimics my internal one as we both turn to see smoke rising near the main building.

"Let's go," I say, running down the stairs over to the next house where Dalton and Marcus are already coming outside.

"Get in the truck, we're under attack," Dalton calls.

"I don't have any gear yet," I say, climbing into the back seat next to Kee. Marcus is handing her gear and putting it on his own.

"It's okay, We'll get you sorted when we get there." Dalton is in battle mode. There's a fierceness that comes over his face as we draw closer to where the explosion happened.

"*Fuck*, Luke was at the armory," I whisper, looking over to Kee.

Reaching over she squeezes my hand. "I'm sure he's fine. Luke can take care of himself; he's trained for this type of thing."

We pull into the main building at the same time as Mika and John. There are other team members around that I don't recognize, but I nod to Gray as they arrive.

I look over to where the armory is, looking for Luke. I can see his truck, but I don't see him.

"Where's Luke?" I ask Mika as he walks up to our group.

"He's inside, he's fine. Your gear is in there with him. Why don't you go get suited up?"

I leave the group and hurry inside of the main building, needing to see Luke and make sure that he's okay.

"Luke?" I call out as I enter the building. I can't keep the shaking out of my voice.

"In here!"

I walk into the monitoring room and there he is. I try not to rush over, but I can't help myself. I meet him halfway across the room, holding him at arm's length as I look over his body. My legs feel wobbly as I grasp onto him.

"You're alright?"

"Yeah, it was close, but it missed me. I'm fine, I promise. See?" Luke pulls away and does a slow spin for me. "I'm alright." Taking my shaking hand, he puts it over his heart. Feeling the steady thumping calms me. I look over him again before stepping away and taking a steadying breath.

"Here, let's get your armor on." Luke's voice is soft and full of patience and understanding.

"I was worried about you, worried the explosion was the armory."

"I know, I'm sorry I scared you." Luke's hands move deftly over my armor as he straps me into the vest, yet they linger as he comes to the straps over my shoulders. He pauses long enough to rest his forehead against mine, taking steadying breaths with me.

"Did you see where the RPG came from?" I whisper as he pulls away, finishing buckling my vest.

"I just caught a glimpse of it as it went by. It happened too quickly for me to see where it came from." Luke is moving as he speaks, handing me a pistol for my sidearm and loading an automatic rifle for me to use as well.

"Why haven't they fired again? What are they waiting for?" The uncertainty in our situation makes my anxiety worsen. I try to keep it in check, but having Luke in harm's way changes the situation for me.

"I know. It makes me think they're waiting to see what our response is."

"What is our response?" I ask, looking at Luke as he hands me the AR, our hands brushing briefly during the exchange.

"I'm not sure what Mika will want to do. The goal is to keep us all in the compound for as long as possible. We don't want to take the fight to them because it will leave us exposed. The woods outside of the compound are probably crawling with Dimitri's men."

Luke moves to leave the room. "Wait. Promise me you'll be careful out there," I say, reaching for his hand.

"I'll do my best, James. I promise. You do the same." He takes a step and our lips lock in a heated kiss, all passion and zero finesse.

I struggle to get my wits about me as Luke pulls back from the bruising kiss with a smile on his face.

"We need to get out there before they think we got lost."

All I can do is nod and follow Luke out of the armory.

As we step out, we're greeted by the rest of the team and Mika's voice.

"Alright, Dalton and John are going to the main gate to make sure Dimitri and his men can't gain access. If they need backup, Marcus and I will go. Gray, Luke, and James will stay here as a final line. I'll split up the rest of the team between Dalton and myself. Be smart and stay safe. If you need help, call out over the comms. Everyone good to go?" Mika looks around the group.

"Affirmative," I call out with the rest of the team.

Gray, Luke, and I watch as the rest of the team head off to their areas. Now, we hunker down and wait. Hopefully, we won't be needed, but I have a bad feeling that this is just Dimitri playing with us.

I glance at Luke as he takes cover behind a pickup and I follow suit, stationing behind an SUV opposite him. He glances over and the sun reflects in his cornflower blue eyes, making them shimmer for a moment before he looks away. Gray takes cover next to

Luke, most likely because of his leg. This way, if he needs to move quickly, Gray can lend a hand and offer cover.

A tense silence settles over the compound as we wait for Dimitri's next move, it goes on for several minutes when suddenly Mika's voice comes over the radio.

"Everyone get ready. We've got movement in the trees outside of the compound."

I take a deep, steadying breath and check my weapon, ensuring it's ready to go. I look over at Luke and Gray and catch Luke's eyes. He gives me a nod and a tight smile. I return it and wish that I was over there with him. I should be there, not Gray, but the truth is that I'm a liability. For several reasons, one being that I only have one hand. I'd hate to slow Luke down or not be able to help because of my broken arm.

I take another breath and wait for the chaos to hit.

The silence is almost deafening until it's shattered by the whistling sound that I'm all too familiar with. Rocket-propelled grenades come singing through the air through the gate. I can see the trails from where I'm set up and all I can do is hope that they miss everyone on the front line.

Chaos erupts over the comms as Dalton, John, and someone named Garrett defend the front gate as Dimitri's men swarm from the trees. The soft popping of gunfire means that they've engaged with them at the front gate. It's only a matter of time before they breach the gates and infiltrate the compound.

As if on cue, John's voice announces over the radio that the gates are gone and that the rest of us should get ready. I check my weapon again, flip the safety off, and mentally prepare myself for what's coming our way.

The sound of gunfire draws closer along with the sounds

of revving vehicles. Dimitri's men are past the second line and headed our way. I look to Luke and Gray again, meeting both of their glances as we prepare our aim.

The first vehicle comes barreling down the dirt road, kicking up gravel and snow as it races towards us. Luke opens fire first, shooting in short, well-placed bursts. He aims first at the driver and then at the block of the SUV, hoping to disable the vehicle. I follow suit and aim for the front tires, taking measured shots to not waste ammo. Gray takes up shooting the driver's side.

The SUV comes to a screeching halt about fifty feet from us and the occupants jump out, scattering for cover as we continue to fire at them. The sound of several RPGs launching at the front draws my attention for the briefest moments before I return to firing at the man closest to me.

Bullets start pinging off the SUV, making me take cover—they've got a bead on me. I rotate to my left and open fire as one of the men makes a run to get around the SUV I'm behind. His body spasms erratically as my shots make contact, jerking him around as if he were a marionette doll and I the puppet master. He falls dead at the trunk of the SUV. I turn my attention back to the remaining four men who are still firing at Luke, Gray, and me.

I glance at Luke and Gray and see they've killed two more of Dimitri's men, leaving only two behind. My heart roars in my ears as I aim at the nearest man and pray that we're all going to make it out of this.

Until a new burst of gunfire draws my attention back to the road.

Shit.

Three new vehicles are racing towards us and it doesn't look like anyone from the compound is in pursuit. The radios have been silent for a minute or two and I'm beginning to worry. The new batch of vehicles pulls to a stop and men pile out. *We are so screwed.* We're outnumbered and outgunned.

Luke calls out over the radio, "We need backup over here, now!"

"We're on our way!" comes Mika's response.

Our shots become less precise and grouped as we split our attention between multiple targets. The SUV I'm taking cover behind is getting hammered by Dimitri's men and I will have to move to a new location soon.

I look over at Luke and Gray and know they're in the same situation.

"Luke, we need to move!" I call out over the sound of gunfire.

He stops firing and ducks behind the truck as Gray continues to fire, keeping Dimitri's men at bay.

Another whistle fills the air and an RPG hits between Mika's team and where we are. Dirt and debris are tossed through the air, peppering our team and Dimitri's. It's obvious that he doesn't care who survives, just as long as he gets his revenge.

I freeze for a moment in the aftermath of the explosion and let the feeling of panic wash through me. I get back to my knees and start shooting at Dimitri's men again, giving Gray a chance to reload. Luke is looking around for a place for us to fall back to, but it's looking like using the buildings for cover might be our only choice.

"James! Can you make it to us?" Luke calls.

"Cover me!" I shout back, readying myself to sprint across the open space between the vehicles.

Luke and Gray pop up and open fire, laying down cover as I take off across the space. I dig my boots into the gravel as I try to gain traction and speed as fast as possible. The dirt kicks up around me as bullets slam into the hard, frozen ground. If I make this, it'll be a fucking miracle.

I throw myself the last couple of feet, hoping that I'll land somewhere behind the truck and not be riddled with bullet holes. As I hit the solid, cold ground, the breath is knocked from my desperately heaving lungs. I grunt out in pain, landing hard on my broken arm.

I could have done that a little better, I think with a wince.

"James!" Luke grabs me and pulls me the rest of the way behind the truck so I'm between him and Gray. I try to catch my breath, but struggle.

"Are you hit? James, are you hit!"

All I can do is shake my head and manage, "Breath… knocked out…"

I lean my head back against the truck and try to catch my breath. "I'm good," I say and run a hand quickly down my body, completely shocked that I made it across without a single bullet hole.

Luke glances over my body, follows my hand, and shakes his head in amazement.

"Where are we falling back to?" I ask.

"It's gonna have to be that outbuilding there." I follow Luke's gaze.

There's a small, brick building not far from us, but far enough that getting there is going to be nearly impossible.

I look at Luke then to Gray. "How are you going to get there?"

"I'm not. I'm going to stay here, provide cover for you two, and hold them back for as long as possible," Luke says, resolute.

"Luke, no. That's not going to work for me. I'll provide cover for you and Gray and then I'll follow. You're going to need help with your leg, I can run fine. I'm not going to leave you behind. I won't argue over this, either."

The three of us look at each other and the decision is made. Gray will take Luke, and I'll provide cover fire.

We're preparing for our next move when the world explodes in flames before going dark.

CHAPTER 12

Luke

Pain flares as the world comes back into focus.

James.

I roll over onto my stomach and lift myself onto my elbows. It takes a moment for my brain to catch up with the rest of my body. An RPG or grenade must have hit near us. I look around and see Gray lying to my right and James just to my left. Neither of them move and the voices of Dimitri's men are getting closer.

"James! James. I need you to get up." I move to get behind the truck, only to realize it's no longer there. Pieces of what was once our truck litter the ground around us.

I can't believe we're all still alive.

I reach for James, only to have a boot slam down on my outstretched hand.

Crying out in pain, I roll, pulling my hand free and swiping out at the foot. Dimitri's man falls and I'm on him in a second, my knife slicing deftly across his exposed throat.

I scramble to get to my feet only to be knocked back down as more of Dimitri's men descend upon us. I'm roughly shoved onto my back then rolled over, as they bind my hands behind my back.

They aren't here to kill us.

One of the men roughly rolls James over. Everything in my body tries to break free as I get a glimpse of his blood and dirt-covered face. I can't do anything—I'm completely useless with my hands tied behind my back. I glance at Gray and see that they're conscious, but don't seem to be fully aware of what's going on with both of their hands already tied in front of them.

I turn back to James, willing him to wake up. They haven't tied his hands because of his cast and I need him to wake up. I need him to be okay.

"James," I whisper as Dimitri's men discuss their next moves.

"James, please. Wake up." I try to move towards him and am met with a boot to the upper back, pinning me to the ground.

Mika's voice erupts over the radio, "Luke, we're coming to you."

Dimitri's men quiet and then it's a rush of movement. They're hauling us all to our feet while one of them lifts James over their shoulder, his limp body swaying with their movement. He leaves behind a trail of blood as they carry him towards the vehicles.

That's when I notice that the sound of gunfire has stopped, which means that we've likely taken out Dimitri's men. Especially if Mika is heading this way. I need him to get here faster. I have to stall.

I pretend like my legs have given out on me, stumbling forward and going to my knees. Dimitri's men are on me immediately. Gray follows suit, pretending to fall, going down to their knees, then stomach, going limp as Dimitri's men try to get them back to their feet.

I can hear vehicles in the distance and I can only pray that it's Mika and the rest of the team. *Please be Mika.*

The man carrying James is at their SUV and has the back door open when Mika and the rest of the team pull up.

"Don't move, no one move!" Mika yells as he, Dalton, John, and Neko get out of the vehicle. Guns are trained on Dimitri's men. There's a tense second and then Dimitri's men open fire. I roll to Gray and the two of us manage to gain our feet and get behind the vehicle in front of us, losing sight of James in the process.

"Mika! Watch out for James!" It's all I can do to let them know that a friend is in the line of fire. I have no idea if he heard, but I hope James has some cover out there.

As suddenly as the gunfire starts, it ends.

I peek out from behind the front of the vehicle and see Mika. All of Dimitri's men are dead. *I have to get to James.* I struggle against the zip ties binding my wrists, bursting free of them as soon as Gray cuts them away.

I stumble out from behind the SUV and limp over to where James is lying in a heap, half in and half out of the vehicle. I can't hear anything around me. My sole focus is on James. Getting to him and making sure he's okay is all I care about. I ignore Mika yelling at me to stay put, ignore Gray's grabbing hands, and rush to James.

His face is ashen and vibrant red from the blood still oozing from the wound on his temple. I reach for his neck to feel for a pulse, almost passing out when I do feel one. It's there and it's steady. He's unconscious and probably concussed again, but he's breathing. My hands are shaking as I grasp James by the shoulder and waist, lowering him slowly to the ground.

"Neko! I need Neko!" I call out, hearing the panic in my own voice as if it weren't mine. I try to steady my breathing as I hold

James' head on my lap and push his hair back from his bleeding forehead.

Movement catches my attention and I look up to see Neko rushing towards me. He's got his kit with him and is covered in grime from being on the frontline earlier.

"Let me see him, Luke." Neko drops to his knees next to us and checks James' pulse and pupils.

"Let's take him to the medical center so Hannah can examine him."

Between us, we manage to get James up and start towards the medical center. Breathing is suddenly hard as my chest tightens with concern.

"How did we come out?" I ask Neko.

"Garrett got caught by some shrapnel, but he's going to be okay. Other than that, he has minor cuts and bruises. James and Garrett are the two who got it the worst."

"He's going to be alright, right, Neko? Should we be worried that he hasn't woken up?"

"It will probably take him a bit to come around. It'll be best to have Hannah look him over, though."

"Fuck, Neko. He was already concussed. I'm worried."

"He'll be alright, Luke. You need to get looked at, too."

"What are you talking about?" I look down at myself and am surprised to see blood seeping from several smaller wounds across my chest and abdomen. *Shrapnel.*

"I'm fine, I don't feel anything."

"Yeah, it's called adrenaline, you idiot." Neko glances at me, shaking his head.

We get to the medical center and are met by Hannah and Lance, another member of the team.

"Oh, James," Hannah says as she reaches us. "Put him over there. Luke, you can take the bed next to him."

"Garrett's on his way here as well," Neko says as he helps me lay James down on the bed.

I stay next to James' bed, not wanting to leave him until he wakes up and knows where he is. I don't want him to wake up and be alone.

"Luke, you need to sit down at least. You're losing blood and I won't have you bleeding all over the place."

"Fine, but I'm not leaving James' side."

Hannah rolls her eyes at me as she starts to look James over. Hannah and Neko remove James' clothes, leaving him just in his boxer briefs. I can't help but look his entire body over. He's got new cuts scattered over his body, but the head wound is the worst of it. Hannah cleans the wound and starts stitching it closed. James doesn't move at all as she works on him, making me more and more concerned for him. They wheel him away briefly to run a few scans to ensure that he doesn't have brain damage after receiving multiple concussions.

Once they've seen James, and Hannah assures me that he's fine, I let Hannah tend to my wounds as she cleans and dresses them. I'm lucky in that nothing is serious; they're all flesh wounds.

"Okay, you're all patched up. Let me know when James wakes up. I'm going to see if anyone else needs assistance." Hannah walks away and I slip my now-holey shirt on and reach for James' hand, hoping that the physical touch will bring him around.

I squeeze and am relieved to feel him squeeze my hand back. I study his cut and bruised face, noticing that his eyes are moving behind the lids.

I hope it's a good dream.

CHAPTER 13

James

t's the same dream that I always have. But this time, I know I'm dreaming.

Even as I walk towards the bloody, mangled body on the ground in front of me, I'm aware that this is all a dream, that it's not real. The panic, pain, and fear are all too real, though, and I can't stop myself from walking to Shawn. Every fiber of my being is calling out for him, pulling me to him.

Kneeling, I pull his body towards my lap and gaze at his bloodied face. His features are twisted in a final moment of agony that is forever seared into my brain. His right arm is gone below the elbow, leaving behind a jagged stump; his right leg at mid-thigh is in a similar state. He's losing too much blood and there's nothing I can do.

It's already too late, anyway. There's a dullness to his once-sparkling eyes that lets me know that he's already gone. His life seeps into the ground around us.

My grief is overwhelming and steals my breath before bursting from my aching lungs, taking flight as I scream Shawn's name over and over until my throat is raw and I taste blood.

The soft pressure of someone squeezing my hand briefly pulls me from my grief long enough for me to remember that this is just a dream. I grasp the pressure, squeezing back and gripping it, anchoring myself to reality.

Please don't leave me here.

I try to open my eyes, but can't quite manage. They're so heavy, my whole body is. The panic grows and I squeeze harder, not letting go of the pressure that squeezes back.

"James?"

Luke's voice breaks apart the clouds of confusion and grief that blanket my mind. The pressure becomes recognizable as his hand.

"James, can you hear me?" Luke asks again.

How many times has he had to ask me that in the last week?

I try to open my eyes again and am relieved when they do. One after another opens slowly. Blinking, I try to clear the fog and gritty feeling from my eyes as the room slowly becomes focused.

Luke's face is the first thing I see.

He's got small cuts all over his face and a few bruises are starting to pop up on one side of his face. His shirt is filthy and covered in small holes and some blood.

"Hey," is all I can manage to say as I clear my thoughts, trying to shake off the nightmare. It's getting easier to recover after I wake up, but the vision of Shawn's broken body still lingers as I look at Luke.

"Hey, yourself. You took another good knock to the head. How ya feeling?"

Sitting up slowly, I take stock of my body and am pleasantly surprised to find that although I have a headache, the rest of my body feels relatively fine.

"I actually feel pretty good, considering." I reach over, putting a finger through one of the larger holes in Luke's shirt, and raise an eyebrow.

"Just some scratches," he says with a wink, then leans forward and kisses my mouth before I can protest.

He pulls away slowly with his hand remaining on my face. I'm immediately lost in the ocean of his eyes—so much so that I don't see Hannah walk up until she clears her throat.

"Sorry to interrupt, but I need to check on my patient; I think he may have hit his head harder than I initially thought." She's smirking and her cheeks are about as red as mine.

Luke leans back, settling on the edge of the bed while grinning at Hannah. "I would beg to differ; I think he's finally in his right mind."

"I'm right here," I say, looking between them and rubbing a hand over my face to hide my disbelief and embarrassment.

Hannah gives Luke a slight shove and shines a light in one eye after the other.

"I think it's safe to say that you're probably a bit concussed, but not nearly as bad as the last time. Keep the wound clean and we can remove the stitches in a week or so. We'll see how it heals."

"Thanks, Hannah. I'll try to avoid being blown up again until then."

"Please do." She smiles at me and touches my shoulder softly. "You two can get out of here when you're ready. I'll grab you some of the scrubs lying around so you're not out there in your boxers."

"Hey, how's Garrett doing?" Luke asks before Hannah can get too far.

"He's getting plenty of stitches and some staples, but he'll be alright. Now, worry about yourself and James. I've got my hands full enough with the rest of the team and Gray." Hannah grins again, leaving briefly before returning with a set of scrubs for me to wear back to Luke's.

"Thanks, Hannah. For everything," I say again, giving her a meaningful look.

"Of course, James." She pats my hand on her way out.

"Let's get you home," Luke says, helping me get into my scrubs.

I'm a bit unsteady as I stand up, but Luke steadies me on his one good leg as best he can.

"Do we have a plan going forward? Dimitri isn't going to give up so easily," I say as we leave the medical center, and I get a look at the grounds of the compound. There are craters where RPGs have hit, debris everywhere, and several vehicles that have been destroyed. Not to mention the numerous bodies of Dimitri's men lying scattered throughout the battleground.

"How does Mika plan to explain all of this to the local authorities?"

"Mika is well-known to the authorities, from both local and federal agencies in the area. They have a good working relationship and sometimes the federal agencies use the Feather Flight Group to assist on missions. I assume they've already contacted them about what happened today and the authorities are on the way," Luke says as he opens the door to a new vehicle that is not riddled with bullet holes.

"That's pretty fucking impressive," I mutter, getting into the passenger seat.

"No kidding. Mika's built an amazing business and team here. Now, we need to protect it."

Luke turns the truck around and we head to his house at the back of the compound. It's like a whole other world at the end of the long drive. It's peaceful back here, the houses untouched by the events that happened at the gates earlier in the day.

"Are you tired?" Luke asks, pulling up to his house and putting the truck in park.

"Not really. The opposite, actually. I'm a bit wired. Why?"

"I plan to get you naked as soon as we get in the house. If that's not something you want, then you need to tell me now because once I start, I don't think I'll be able to stop, James."

Luke's proclamation makes me freeze with my hand on the door handle of the truck. My heart rate kicks into high gear. He's so bold, I don't know what to do or say. Shawn was the opposite of Luke when it came to his pursuits. I've never been with anyone like Luke before.

I swallow and open the truck door, get out, and start walking towards the house without saying a word or looking at Luke. If I don't have the words to express myself right now, I guess actions will have to do.

I wait at the door for Luke and smile to myself, hearing the door quickly opening and closing, the fall of his hurried, uneven footsteps coming towards me.

I wait until he's close, then open the door and walk inside. I can feel his warmth and presence behind me as I enter the house. I'm holding my breath as he closes the door behind me and let it out when he reaches out, grabbing my arm and pulling my back to meet his chest.

His erection presses into my lower back and I start to get hard in response to how badly he wants me.

"You had me worried today," he whispers into my ear as he brushes his lips across the side of my neck, his facial hair gently caressing my warming flesh.

I don't say anything, but I lean more into his chest, feeling his solid body behind me and allowing him to continue kissing my neck from behind.

Luke moves so that he's standing in front of me, pressing me against the door. His kisses are soft brushes against my neck and jaw. Then he hovers over my lips, mere inches away. If I move just a bit, our lips will touch. He breathes out as I breathe in, his eyes glued to my lips as he lightly brushes his lips against mine. His hand caresses the places where his lips just touched, leaving a burning trail of heat behind.

He draws me closer with a hand to the back of my neck, gently guiding me into his space as he rocks against me. Our hard bodies come together as our arousal grows.

"Do you want me, James?" Luke's voice is almost as gentle as his kisses as he grazes my jaw with his lips again.

I nod.

"Say it. Say you want me, James."

"I…want you, Luke," I whisper the words. His grip on the back of my neck tightens as he pulls me in for a bruising kiss. His tongue parts my lips as I gasp, feeling his hard cock pressing into my abs. My own arousal is so hard that it's painful.

The feeling of Luke kissing me takes over every part of my body, consuming my mind until there's nothing left but the sensation of his lips on mine, his hands on my neck and in my hair, and his body against mine.

I pull away, leaning my head back and giving Luke access to my neck. He takes it and immediately starts kissing from my jaw down, lingering there for a moment before reaching down for the hem of my shirt.

"Can I?" he asks breathlessly.

All I can do is nod and blink the haze away as he pulls my shirt up and over my head, making sure not to jostle my head or arm too much. Luke is all hard planes, but he's so gentle in how he touches and talks to me. It's like he knows just what I need to be comfortable.

I lean my head back again as Luke returns to kissing my neck the moment my shirt is off. He kisses down my neck to my chest, taking a hard nipple in his mouth and flicking it with his tongue. I groan and tangle my hands in his hair, taking a handful of his blonde locks and pressing him closer to my nipple. I revel in the lightning shooting through my body with each flick of his tongue.

Luke continues moving down my body, his hands replacing the places his tongue just was. I'm panting by the time he reaches the waistline of the scrubs I'm wearing. He tugs them down and I'm soon completely naked, leaning against the door.

Luke kisses from the base of my shaft to the tip before taking me fully into his mouth, sucking me to the back of his throat.

"Ahhh, fuck Luke," a broken whisper pours from my lips as his tongue cradles my cock.

"Do you like that?" Luke whispers back, licking down the length of me.

"Yes, yes," I mumble incoherently, letting my hips rock forward with the motion of his mouth and hand.

"Do you want me to keep going?"

"Please…" I'm practically begging him at this point.

"Come with me." Luke pulls away and the chilly air of the foyer hits my flushed skin.

Luke grabs my hand and leads me to the living room where he puts down a blanket on the leather sofa. He pushes me down and kneels between my legs.

"I love the way you taste," he breathes.

"Luke…"

I grasp his messy hair as he sucks me into the warmth of his mouth again. This time, I don't hold back, letting my hips thrust in time with Luke's sucking. I'm completely lost in the feeling of him, desperately willing myself not to cum as I don't want it to be over yet.

"James, I want to fuck you," Luke whispers softly between the flicks of his tongue on the tip of my dick.

"Yes…please, Luke." I can't stop myself. I'm consumed with my desire, my *need* for Luke.

He crawls up my body, peppering it with sloppy kisses from his swollen lips as he asks me the question I'm dying to hear: "You want me to fuck you, James?"

"Yes," I pant.

"Are you sure?"

"Yes, Luke, I need you," I beg.

Luke moans into my chest as I wrap my hand around his throbbing dick.

"Please…fuck me."

CHAPTER 14

Luke

almost come undone at James' pained whisper.

I continue to prowl up his body, kissing every inch of him on my way before our lips meet in a frenzy of needy kisses.

James is desperately trying to get my pants off while also trying to keep one hand on my engorged dick.

I reach down between us, helping his fumbling hands undo the button and zipper of my pants. James reaches into my pants and pulls my cock free of my shorts.

Then does the hottest thing I've ever seen him do.

James leans in and spits on my dick, running his hand smoothly over my length.

My hips buck on their own and James tightens his hold. The friction builds and I thrust harder into his hand.

"Mmm, James. Damn, baby, that feels good." I suck his earlobe, loving the way he's panting as I kiss him.

"Luke, please fuck me." I can tell James is close. I want to make our first time last. I'm not quite sure if I'm ready to fuck him just yet.

"I will, James, soon." I pull away, removing my clothes so I'm completely naked. James' eyes drink me in, the amber darkening with lust and want as he takes in my body, settling on my hard length.

"Suck my cock, James." His cheeks redden with heat.

He goes to his knees in front of me, taking me in his mouth to the hilt.

I hold his head in place, fucking his face as he sucks me deeper still until the tip of my dick hits the back of his throat. I keep it there, thrusting hard until he gags around my cock.

"Is this okay, James?"

He nods and continues, his hands gripping each of my ass cheeks as I thrust again and again, driving into his throat. The roughness of his cast adds to the sensations.

"That's good, baby. That feels so good," I praise.

James moans and hums around my dick. I put two fingers in my mouth, wetting them, and bend over James' body, rubbing them over his tight hole. He gasps around my dick as I press the tip of one finger against his entrance.

"Relax, baby," I instruct, pressing a bit harder as I feel him loosen around the pressure of my finger. I slip my finger in, pressing it into his prostate. James pulls away from my cock, calling out my name, resting his head against my thigh as I continue to gently slide my finger back and forth before slipping the second finger in.

"Luke!" James keens, his fingers dig into my thighs. He drops one of his hands to his own dick and begins stroking. He has to be close.

I reach down with my other hand and bat his hand away from his cock, "Not yet, James."

"Please." His voice is a whine, I know he's dying to have my cock inside of him.

"Okay, baby. You've been such a good boy; I'll give you what you want." I pull my fingers free and help James up before bending him over the arm of the sofa.

I spit, slickening his entrance and my dick as I prepare to enter him. I want to go slowly, but everything in my body is dying to be inside him, to be rough.

"Are you ready, baby?" I ask, leaning over his body and kissing the back of his neck and his shoulder.

"Yes, Luke. I need you, please." I love that he wants me so badly.

"So polite, aren't you, James?" I coo.

"Please…" he moans as I press the tip of my dick to his entrance.

"Okay, baby." I lean over him again, kissing his neck as I press the tip of my hard cock into him. He resists at first before relaxing around me. I slide into his warm depths, inch by inch. I'm desperate to slam into him, thrusting myself home, but I know it's been a while for him. I need to go slow until he's ready.

"More, Luke," James moans. I sink in, slowly coming undone with the feel of him around me.

"I don't know how long I'm going to last," I whisper, leaning down and nipping at his broad shoulders, marveling at how his muscles bunch with every slow push of my dick.

"I need you to go faster," James says, looking over his shoulder at me.

"Faster? You're sure?"

"Yes, please, Luke. Go faster," he pleads.

I fill him fully and start slowly thrusting in and out, building momentum, encouraged by his moaning and response as I rock into him. He feels so good tightening around me.

I grip James by the hips and pull out to the tip before thrusting fully into him repeatedly, reveling in the feel and the small sounds he makes with every push of my hips.

James reaches between his legs and strokes himself to the same rhythm as my thrusting. I grab his shoulders and pull him into my body, replacing his hand with mine. I stroke him, using the precum on the tip of his dick as lubricant as I tighten my grip, stroking faster and faster as James leans back into me.

He turns his head and kisses my neck, sucking lightly as I continue to thrust and stroke him. I want him to come first. I want to see him lose control. To let the passion and feelings fully consume him. I need to watch him lose himself.

"Luke…"

James gasps and grips me tighter. I can feel his balls tightening and know he's close.

Good, I'm about to lose my mind, I can't keep going for much longer.

"James, I wanna see you cum, baby. Will you cum for me?" I thrust hard into him, almost knocking the two of us forward onto our hands and knees. James cries out and calls out my name as he comes undone.

I thrust harder and faster, knowing that he's climaxed and desperate for my own release. It doesn't take long before I fall over the edge and follow James into oblivion.

When I come to, the two of us are lying on the rug in front of the fire, completely wasted and drained from our afternoon antics. I roll over and gently shake James awake.

"James, we should take a shower and move to the bed." I shake him again and he slowly stirs, rolling into me and snuggling in.

"No, we should get up. Come on," I urge.

"Let's just stay here a bit longer," he mumbles.

I chuckle at the cuteness—not something that I see a lot of when it comes to James. He comes off as all sharp edges and moodiness, but the truth is that he's hurt and scared, needing someone to help him out. He's more than meets the eye, that's for sure.

"We're getting up. Let's go." I slap his ass to motivate him. Soon we're climbing the stairs naked and heading straight to my room. I start a shower as James leans against the sink, watching me.

"Enjoying the view?" I tease.

James smiles and tracks his eyes up and down my body before answering, "Very much."

I stalk towards him and back him against the sink, kissing him hard.

"If you keep doing that, we'll never make it to the shower," he whispers softly against my already kiss-swollen lips. He presses his forehead into mine before pushing me back from him. Our naked bodies tangle slightly before we both walk into the warm water of the shower.

James sighs as the water hits his body and leans back into me. I love the feeling of his slick skin against mine.

"Are you feeling okay?"

"A little sore...everywhere," he admits.

"You've been through a lot today. I hope I wasn't too rough."

"Not at all. It was great, perfect," James says, still leaning against my body.

I take the soap and lather us both up, taking my time on James' body. I'm mesmerized by the way the water and bubbles wander down the ridges of his body, slowly sliding along the places that I've just touched, that I've just kissed. I follow a trail of suds with my finger as it flows down his chest and abdomen, stopping as it hits the wiry curls of his pubic hair.

James returns the favor by lathering more soap and rubbing my body down, starting at my shoulders. His large hands follow the ridges and valleys of my muscular body. I watch James as he takes his time washing my body. His eyes follow the line of my clavicle before moving to the mounds of my pectoral muscles, then to the valleys of my abdominal muscles, before sweeping back up to my lips.

"You're beautiful," he whispers softly, his eyes glued to my lips.

"So are you, James." I trace my finger along a scar that blemishes his chest before leaning to kiss it. I lift James' chin and kiss him softly.

"Come on, let's rinse off and get some rest." I take the shower head off the holder, bring it closer to us, and start to rinse the suds off our bodies. I love the way that James leans into the warm water.

Stepping out of the shower, I grab a towel and hand it to James before grabbing one for myself.

"I'll be right back," I say, walking to the bedroom door in my towel.

"Where are you going?"

"I'm getting your stuff. There's no reason to keep it in the room down the hall if you're going to be sleeping in here every night."

"Who says I'll be sleeping in here every night?" James raises an eyebrow.

"I mean, you will, won't you?" Suddenly, I'm feeling uncertain and a little awkward for assuming that James would want to keep sleeping with me.

I can see the wheels turning in his head as he thinks it over for a minute before giving me a nod. I head down the hallway to the guest bedroom, grab his unpacked bag of clothes, and bring it back to the room with me where James is waiting in his towel.

I hand him his bag and grab a gray sweatshirt from my dresser. By the time I turn around, James is already dressed in a pair of navy blue sweats and a white T-shirt, sitting on the edge of the bed.

"Whatcha thinking about?" I ask, moving to sit next to him.

"What do you think Dimitri is going to try next?"

"He won't take this hit lying down, that's for sure. We need to make a move soon. I hate just sitting here waiting for him to come at us again." I rest my hand on James' knee and feel some of the tension leave his body.

"Should we check in with Mika before we call it a night?"

"No, if Mika needs us, he'll reach out. The team is bigger than you think. I'm sure there are patrols going day and night that we don't know about. Plus, after today, it's best for us to get some rest and hit the ground running tomorrow."

James reaches out resting his hand atop mine. He's tentative as always, as if he's struggling with what he wants to do and what he thinks he should do.

I turn my hand over and grasp his before he can remove it.

"Should we go to bed?"

"Yeah, that sounds good."

Something's wrong, though; James won't look me in the eye and seems a little distant.

"What's going on?" I ask, gripping his hand tightly as he tries to pull away.

"It's just… What if I have a nightmare? I don't want to wake you."

"I'd rather be here with you and help bring you out of it than it be any other way, James."

James looks into my eyes as if weighing my words.

"I'm here for you, James. There's nowhere else I'd rather be right now. There isn't a bed in this house I'd rather you sleep in. I want you here with me, in my bed."

A flicker of emotion in his brown eyes lets me know he's finally starting to get it.

"I won't be running anywhere, James. No matter how hard you try to scare me away, I'm staying right here." I put my hand back on his thigh and watch as the words sink in.

"Let's go to bed." I stand up, pulling him with me and into a hug before letting him go to pull the covers down.

"Luke…" James pauses, shifting back and forth. "I don't know what I'm doing or who I am right now. I don't know if I have the capacity to give anything back to you…emotionally. What if I can't do that?"

Putting my hand on his shoulder, I pull him in for another hug. "I'm going to say something that you probably don't want to hear, but I think going to therapy again would be really good for you." I pull away and wait for James to get defensive or to tear away from me.

He doesn't move.

"I think you're right." It's a small, quiet admission that makes my heart leap into my throat.

"Yeah? You'd be open to that?"

"Yeah, I'd be open to doing therapy again. I don't *want* to be like this, Luke. I don't *enjoy* being like this. It's just what I've known for so long, I am not sure if this is who I am now. What if it is? What if I can't be fixed?"

"You don't need to be fixed, James. You need help learning how to manage your trauma. It will never go away for good, but with help, you can learn to move past it. To live your life how *you* want to instead of how your *trauma* allows you to."

"I need to do something; I can't keep living like this—one foot in and one foot out."

I reach for James, pulling him into me and kissing him roughly before softening into a slow, sensual kiss.

"I'll help you however I can," I whisper against his lips. I feel him nod into me before leaning in for another kiss.

James kisses me hard this time, like he's desperate to remember what it's like to kiss. Like it's the last time he'll kiss me, like he's saying goodbye.

Pulling away, I pause, looking at him closely. "What was that?"

"Just in case I'm too broken to be fixed," he whispers, the words choking from his throat.

"*You are not broken, James.*" I enunciate each and every word, drilling them home with a kiss that steals his breath. "Now get in bed."

James does as he's told, crawling under the blankets and rolling to his side so he can face me as I walk around to the other side and get under the blankets.

Laying on my side we're face to face, yet there seems to be so much distance between us. It's as if I can feel him pulling away.

"Please don't go anywhere," I whisper.

"I'll try not to. I'll try to stay here...with you," he whispers back.

CHAPTER 15

James

'm gone before he wakes.

Sneaking away in the early morning hours, I walked down the gravel road of the compound's housing block before people started to stir.

The sky is just starting to lighten with the groggy morning sun. My breath is visible in bursts of white fog with every exhale. My boots crunch against the dirt, the only sound in the early morning hours. It fills the air around me, echoing down the road before me, announcing my arrival.

"Thanks for meeting me so early." I walk into the light from the single bulb above the door to the medical unit.

"Of course, anything to help." Mika steps out of the doorway and shakes my outstretched hand.

"I sent a message to the doctor late last night when you reached out. She'll be in later this morning, but I figured we could get you a good breakfast and have you ready for your first session by starting early."

"Thanks, Mika. I mean that." I'm shaking slightly in my coat, a mix of the cold morning air, anxiety, and adrenaline.

"Let's grab some grub." Mika throws a trunk-like arm around my shoulders, and we walk toward the main building.

"Was it Luke?" Mika asks suddenly as we walk into the mess hall.

"Was what Luke?" I ask, preparing myself for some joke or hazing.

"That talked you into getting help?"

"Oh, yeah. He had too many good points to ignore. I've done it before. I guess I thought I had everything under control, but I've just been pushing it down instead of really addressing it."

"You'll like Doctor Hardigan. She has a lot of experience working with folks with PTSD. She's helped many of the guys on the team, including Luke, and I think she will work with Marcus, too."

"Thanks again, Mika." He takes my outstretched hand, gripping it tightly before pulling me into a half hug.

"Alright. Let's eat."

When we walk in, half of the team is already in the cafeteria, chowing down. After yesterday's battle with Dimitri's men, everyone is looking worse for wear. Several of them have cuts and bruises marring their faces and arms. I grab a plate and load up on food, starving from the battle and what Luke and I did later in the living room.

I take a seat next to Mika, Neko, and John. I should have left a note or something for Luke, but I didn't think about it until I was halfway to the main building. I'm not used to thinking about other people's emotions or considering how my actions will affect them. That's going to take some getting used to.

I know I have a lot of work to do, but for the first time in a long time, I'm starting to feel hopeful.

I glance up from my food and lose track of my thoughts as Luke strides into the room, dressed in thigh-hugging jeans, boots, and a red and black flannel. I can't take my eyes off him as he moves through the room, approaching where I sit. His eyes are glued to me.

And he's not happy.

"Someone's in trouble," Neko whispers, snickering beside me.

I put down the half-eaten piece of bacon in my hand and shoot him some side-eye, wishing that people didn't know that there was something going on between us. But I also feel like maybe this is all okay. Perhaps this is how it's supposed to be. Maybe everything will be fine.

"You left early," Luke says, stopping across the table from me.

"I needed to talk with Mika."

"Next time, let me know where you're going. I don't like waking up to an empty bed and not knowing where you are."

I feel heat touching my cheeks and resist the urge to look at Neko and Mika to see their reactions.

"Sorry, I'll leave a note next time."

I feel like he wants to say more, but instead, he gives me a nod and walks away towards the food. I watch him as he goes, transfixed by how his jean-clad leg muscles ripple with every step.

I turn back to my food and catch Mika and Neko exchanging glances. I try to make myself smaller and focus on the food in front of me. I don't look up again until Luke places his plate across from me and sits down without saying a word.

Shit, he's really upset.

"What's the plan for today?" I ask, looking around the table.

Mika rescues me from the awkward silence that follows. "We're figuring out how to deal with Dimitri. He did a number on our defenses, and we've got to make the next move before he hits us again."

"Any ideas on what those entail?" Luke grumbles through a mouthful of eggs and bacon.

"We've got an idea of where he's holed up. A team is being sent out to do some recon today and to get an idea of what we're up against. His numbers surprised us yesterday, and I don't plan on letting that happen again."

"I want on the team," Luke says, looking up from his now empty plate.

"I don't think so," Neko says, pointing to Luke's boot.

"I'll take it off or stay with the transportation. I want in," he says again, looking at Mika.

"I have to agree with Neko. I don't think you should go, you're still healing," Mika says.

Luke opens his mouth, but Mika speaks before he can say anything. "Let me clarify that. You're not going, Luke. That's an order."

Luke slouches back in his chair like a scolded child, crossing his arms and pouting. I turn to Mika, ready to ask, but he cuts me off with a look and I keep the question to myself.

"I mean, they could come and stay in the vehicle as our last-ditch excuse of a rescue team if shit goes sideways," John says without looking up from his plate of mostly bacon, which is a good thing given the death look Mika shoots him.

I nod to show my agreement with John. "We can stay in the vehicles," I reiterate. I can see Luke nodding, his grin growing ever larger as he sees Mika starting to break.

"You guys are like a bunch of children," Mika mutters. "Fine, you two can come along, but you stay in the vehicles and you *do not* leave them, no matter what happens. Are we clear?"

"Clear!" Luke and I respond together. Luke grins at me from across the table and a tingling sensation rolls through my body. I haven't felt that sensation in years. I'm happy, genuinely happy, at this moment. I grin back at Luke and almost laugh out loud when I feel his boot tap mine under the table.

"When do we leave?" Luke asks. He really is like a kid. The excitement radiates off him and he's practically bubbly with the thought of joining the mission.

"This afternoon. We'll head out for some initial recon then we'll decide what to do from there."

"Great, we'll be ready to rock by then." Luke gives me a nod as he gets up, motioning for me to come with him.

I check my watch. "I can't. I've got an appointment in five." I look back up at Luke. He doesn't ask questions, but instead smiles at me.

"Let me know if you want me to pick you up when you're done. Just shoot me a text."

"I can walk."

"Well, in case you don't feel like walking, you can text me and I'll come pick you up."

"Okay, I'll let you know."

I can feel the eyes of everyone at the table tracking our exchange and feel a bit of heat building from my neck to my cheeks. I'm not one to blush, but something about the entire team knowing that Luke and I are shacking up makes me a bit uncomfortable. But they don't react.

Luke smiles, having gotten my confirmation, and wanders off

to get more food. I get up and follow Mika to drop our trays off before we head off to meet Dr. Hardigan at the medical building.

Walking down the dirt road, I spot a bright red Kia Soul that I haven't seen at the compound before parked in front of the medical center.

"That'll be Dr. Hardigan," Mika says, pointing towards the car.

"Flashy," I mumble as we walk up, the crunch of gravel under our boots the only sound echoing through the chilly, mid-morning air.

Mika laughs. "Don't worry, she's down to Earth and a great therapist. You're in good hands. Her office is the last door down the hall on the left. Good luck in there and don't be too hard on yourself."

"Right. Thanks." I shake Mika's outstretched hand and head into the building.

The hall feels like it goes on forever, taking me a minute to get to Dr. Hardigan's door. When I do, I pause. My heart races in my chest and I can already feel the panic. I'm more nervous about this conversation than I am going on a mission. I'd take getting shot at over therapy any day, but I know I need this, especially if I want to continue to see Luke.

Steadying myself, I take a deep breath and knock on the door.

"Hi! I'm Dr. Hardigan, come on in. You're James, right?" She's a bundle of energy, but it's controlled energy unlike Luke's chaotic energy, which seems to come out of nowhere. Dr. Hardigan seems to bounce as she walks around her office, which is decorated in calming colors with pops of brightness.

"Hi, yeah, I'm James. Nice to meet you." I give an awkward half-smile and step into her office.

"Have a seat on that chair over there." She points to the chair in front of an antique-looking writing desk littered with papers. Although her office seems to be in a state of organized chaos, it is still somehow calming.

Dr. Hardigan is older than I am, maybe in her early fifties. Her dark hair, streaked with gray, is piled on top of her head in a loose bun. She's wearing glasses the same color as her car and is dressed in an ankle-length pencil skirt and white blouse. She gives off an air of being energetic yet professional.

"Alright, I know you're probably dreading this, but today is all about getting to know each other and figuring out if we're a good fit. If I'm going to be your therapist, I need to know that you're going to be open to the process and trying the exercises that we discuss. Do you think you'll be up for it?"

"Yes, ma'am. I've done therapy before and had good results. I didn't keep up with it, though. I thought I was good to go, but I'm not."

"Please, call me Dr. Hardigan, none of that *ma'am* stuff. I know that will be hard for you, but ma'am is too formal for me!" She pushes the red glasses up her nose before growing serious and continuing, "Don't be too hard on yourself, James. Dealing with trauma takes time, and it's a continuous process. You don't get rid of it or cure it. You work through it and find ways to manage your reactions to it."

She has a kind smile and caring eyes as she looks at me from across the desk. I relax a bit in the chair and take another deep, calming breath.

"Let's talk about what you're here to work on. Can you share a bit about what's causing your anxiety?"

At first, I'm unsure of what to say or if I'll be able to say anything, but once I start, everything seems to pour out of me. I share the joy of meeting Shawn and falling for him, the stress of keeping it a secret, how that affected our relationship, how we worked around that, and how we found our happiness together. Finally, I share how he died.

I manage to keep my voice steady throughout my recounting of the happiest and saddest days of my life, but I can't stop the tears from accumulating in the corners of my eyes as I look down at my hands.

"I avoid getting close to people because I know they won't be around one day. It's easier to say goodbye to someone when you're not close to them," I finish, looking up at Dr. Hardigan.

"That's not a very fulfilling life, though. It's living with one foot out, always waiting for people to leave," she counters thoughtfully.

"It's worked so far."

"Has it, James? Are you satisfied with your relationships?"

I don't answer immediately, taking in the question and rolling it around in my head before responding, "No, I'm…alone. I'm always alone."

"Do you want to be alone?"

"No, not always."

Dr. Hardigan smiles at me, the corners of her eyes wrinkling. "Tell me, what's changed your mind?"

I look down at my hands again, a feeling of embarrassment rolling over me or maybe shyness.

"I've met someone. Someone that I like and that I want to keep seeing. But I'm afraid I'm too broken to give him anything emotionally. I don't know if I have anything left to give."

"Thank you for sharing that. You're not broken; we never

are. We're healing, and that takes time—time to process, work through how to react, and build back up to where we want to be."

I find myself nodding along with her as she speaks, a tiny speck of hope lighting up in my chest. Maybe I could get back to where I want to be. Maybe there's a chance…

"It sounds like a lot to personally deal with, but I'm confident that I can assist your healing with weekly seasons. Are you game to give it a try?"

"Yes, ma'am."

"Please. Call me Dr. Hardigan or Rachel. No need for ma'am's here," she reiterates.

"Yes, Dr. Hardigan."

She smiles again. "Great! Let's get some time on the books and we'll get started next week." Dr. Hardigan gets up from her chair and reaches the small desk where she pulls out a calendar. "How are Tuesdays at ten in the morning?"

"That should work," I mutter, picking at my cast.

"Wonderful. In the meantime, I'd like you to think about specific things you're interested in discussing. Also, think about when you're feeling the most unbalanced and what triggers those moments."

I'm beginning to feel unbalanced right now, I think as I start to feel overwhelmed by everything.

The silence in the room makes me look up at Dr. Hardigan.

She smiles knowingly. "I think that will be it for now." Her voice softened, clearly picking up on my discomfort.

"We're already done?" I ask, checking my watch and surprised that it's already been an hour.

"Yup, you're free to go!"

"Thank you, Dr. Hardigan. It felt good to talk about it."

She smiles and ushers me towards the door.

As she opens it, she reaches out, patting my arm. "Hang in there, James, and try not to let fear control the decisions you're making."

I nod again and start down the hall.

Walking in the cold air helps to clear my head as I start back towards Luke's house at the end of the drive. I'm feeling surprisingly good. It felt nice to talk to someone and to leave feeling so… light.

I reach the house's door and open it. The smell of something delicious immediately fills the air around me.

There's music playing from the kitchen, and I can hear the clanking of dishes. I walk quietly toward the noise, my breath catching as I glimpse Luke in the kitchen. He's completely in his element.

He's still in his tight jeans that hug his thighs and ass perfectly, but he's ditched his heavy sweater for a plain white t-shirt that shows his abdomen when he raises his arms. He's got slippers on his feet and an oven mitt in each hand as he takes a pan out.

He's got a pot of chili on the stove, and the toasted bread he just took from the oven looks absolutely delicious.

I step into the kitchen, wrapping my arms around him from behind. He must have known I was watching because he was not surprised. He leans into my hug before turning in my arms to give me a peck on the lips, brushing his lightly against mine. He tastes like chili powder.

"Did you have a good meeting?" he softly whispers against my lips.

I lean closer, kissing him softly. "Mmhmm, it went well."

"I'm glad to hear that." He stands in my embrace, our lips parting slightly between sweet, slow kisses.

"Are you hungry?" Luke asks, stealing another kiss.

"Famished." I press my growing erection against him.

"Mm, if only we could. If I take you to bed now, I'm afraid we'll never leave. We've got some recon to do."

Disappointed but understanding, I nod and kiss Luke before letting go. "Then let's eat some of this amazing food you've made."

Lunch goes by quickly and before I know it, Luke and I are heading back out towards the main building, dressed in our tactical gear. I'm uneasy as we walk towards the team. I've got a bad feeling about going on this mission, and it's not just because Luke is also going. We're not prepared enough to get so close to Dimitri. The goal is to learn more, but what if it becomes a shootout? Are we ready for that? Am I?

CHAPTER 16

Luke

I can tell James is nervous by the tick in his jaw as he tightens his muscles repeatedly. The more time I spend around him, the more I start to recognize the little things that give away his true emotions; like the way he runs his hands down his thighs when he's unsure or the way he arches his eyebrow when he's trying not to talk back.

I reach for his hand as we walk up the road to where the rest of the team is waiting by our vehicles. I link our fingers loosely together.

"There's nothing to be nervous about," I softly whisper, leaning my shoulder into his.

"You don't know that. They could be expecting us. Anything could happen." James won't look at me, but instead keeps his eyes forward on the team.

"So why worry about it? We will handle whatever comes our way."

"That's a good way to end up dead, Luke. How have you survived this long?" He finally turns his whiskey eyes on me and I give him a huge smile.

"I'm just lucky like that, I guess." I can't help but laugh as he rolls his eyes and tries to pull away from me.

I squeeze his hand before letting go and we join the rest of the team. Mika gives both of us a look and we straighten up. I wipe the smile off my face and focus.

"Alright, you've got your orders. I'm expecting you all to keep to the plan. We get in, we gather what information we can, and we get out. Luke and James, you two are going to ride with me, and you'll be staying with the vehicles during the mission. At *no point* will you engage." Mika gives each of us a pointed look. Seemingly satisfied with what he sees, he continues.

"Alright, let's get going." Mika clasps several of the team on their shoulders as we disperse. The three of us climb into Mika's SUV and lead the way out of the compound.

The location where we think Dimitri is holed up is almost two hours away, but we ride in comfortable silence. I glance a few times at James in the back seat to find him staring thoughtfully out the SUV window, watching the landscape fly by. We're taking back roads to avoid city traffic and to be less conspicuous. Nothing draws attention like a caravan of five black SUVs.

It's late afternoon when we arrive at a seemingly abandoned warehouse complex. It was once a bustling steel factory, but now it's nothing more than decaying brick buildings and rusted machinery. There's a new padlock on the closest gate and the roads are well-traveled, giving away that someone has been here recently.

Mika continues past the property gate for another mile before pulling over and killing the engine. "We get out here and hoof it in," Mika says through the comms.

I glance in the side mirror of the SUV, watching as the doors open in unison and the team starts to assemble outside of their vehicles. I'm dying to go with them. I hate that I have to stay here and can't be with them or help them if they get in trouble. A hand on my shoulder breaks me out of my spiral.

"They'll be fine," James says from the back seat.

I lay my hand on top of his and we stay like this as the team starts up the hill towards the abandoned factory.

"We'll stay on the comms and be ready in case they need us. If shit really hits the fan, we can each take a vehicle and go get them," James says softly, squeezing my shoulder before opening the back door.

I watch as he walks around the front of the vehicle to the driver's side. Damn, he looks good in tactical gear. The dark material hugs him in all the right places, making his arm muscles pop and shoulders wider. I can't take my eyes off him as he opens the door and climbs into the driver's seat.

As James sits down, he looks over and catches me watching him. "What?"

"Nothing, just enjoying the view," I say with a smirk and wink.

His dusky skin tinges red and he turns all of his attention to the small, two-way radio transceiver sitting between us, turning the volume up.

"We should stay focused," James mutters without looking at me.

"Oh, I'm focused." I lean in and nuzzle the side of his neck, the scruff on his jaw tickling my cheek.

"Luke, I mean it. We need to focus. This is serious."

I give his neck a quick peck before sitting back in my seat and checking the mirrors to ensure that we're still alone.

"It's all clear, boss," I tease him, pleased when he glares at me through his dark lashes.

The radio is silent, which is protocol for the team. They're only supposed to use the comms if they run into trouble. The Feather Flight Team has been together for years and has done countless missions. We have our own language based on military tactical hand signals that allow us to communicate without needing to speak. I can almost envision the team moving up on the factory right now, splitting into two groups as they approach the first of the buildings and using signs to relay what they see.

My leg starts to bounce as my desire to be a part of the action grows. It's just a recon mission, but intel and recon are what I'm good at; it's what I do. I should be there with them. We should be using all of our tools right now, including our drone, but we're not and I don't like it.

James places his hand on my bouncing leg and suddenly, the roles have been reversed. I'm usually the one comforting him, but here he is, comforting me as I anxiously wait to hear something over the radio.

"Tell me about yourself, about your old team," James' voice cuts through the comfortable silence that we've been sitting in for the last several minutes.

"Oh man, I loved those guys. They were really great. We were inseparable in and out of the field."

"What happened?" James' eyes follow my every move.

"We were on a mission and had some bad intel. It went sideways fast. We were outmanned and outgunned. Only a few of us made it out and those of us that did retired after that mission."

"I'm sorry, Luke. That's terrible." James reaches across the cab of the SUV and runs his hand down my arm, gently reaching for my hand.

I clasp his fingers in mine and try to block out the visions of that day as they fight to gain control in my mind. "It was hard for a long time, but with help from the Feather Flight Group, it's gotten better. A little easier to handle."

"I'm glad that they were there for you." James doesn't pull back from my hand but squeezes it instead.

An hour passes in silence as James and I sit in the SUV, holding hands while we wait and watch.

There's a crackle over the radio and then it bursts to life.

"We've got contact!" John shouts over the radio, as I hear the pop of gunfire in the background.

"Fuck." I look over at James, who has leaned forward to hear better. I pick up the radio and hold it between us.

"We're on our way to you." Mika's calm, authoritative voice sounds small coming through the receiver.

"Make it quick—" John's voice is cut off by a loud explosion. I get out of the vehicle and look to the east where I last saw my teammates, seeing a large cloud of smoke rising over the hill.

"James…" I look at him.

"I know, let's go." He's already starting the SUV. Slamming the passenger door shut, I jog awkwardly in my boot to the car behind ours and peel out, following closely behind James.

The only thing I can hear is the beating of my heart in my ears and the sound of the tires on the gravel road. James doesn't even pause before ramming the gate and destroying the shiny, new padlock.

I haven't heard anything else come over the comms and the silence makes me even more worried. James follows the factory complex's dirt roads towards the smoke cloud, taking the corners dangerously fast.

I round a particularly sharp corner and almost rear-end James' SUV which has slid to a stop sideways in the road, blocking my view of what's happening. The driver-side door has already been flung open, and James is taking cover behind the front tire, rifle in hand.

I fling open the door, greeted by the sound of gunfire. I rush out to take cover behind James' vehicle with him and grab another rifle from the back seat of his SUV.

"What's the situation?" I ask breathlessly.

"Looks like John's team is pinned down and Mika's team was hit with an RPG, I think. I don't have a visual on them, but I think they're behind that rubble where the smoke is coming from."

"Any idea where Dimitri's men are?"

"I think they're set up in the building across from John's team. They're taking potshots at them any time someone tries to move."

"Alright, let's lay down some fire on the front of the building and see if John's team can evacuate."

James nods his agreement, and we shift to the back of the vehicle, where we have a clear view of the building where Dimitri's men are. I relay the message on the radio to John and the rest of the Feather Flight Team to get everyone squared away.

I give James the signal and he opens fire on the building. As brick and wood splinter from the bullet impacts, the gunfire shifts from where the team is hunkered down to our SUV. James pops back behind the vehicle as bullets ping off it. I run to the front of the vehicle as fast as I can with my boot and motion for John and his team to move.

John signals back to me and starts sending his men over as

James continues to use systematic bursts of fire to keep Dimitri's men occupied. We still haven't heard anything from Mika and his men, but we need to solve one problem at a time. Once we have all of John's team in my SUV, we can figure out how to approach Mika's team. The main concern is ensuring we keep Dimitri's men distracted.

I glance behind me at James to see him ducking down again as the bullets ping off the SUV, ringing through the smokey air around us. Now that John and his team are with us behind the vehicle, I risk a glance over it to see if I can pinpoint where the gunfire is coming from. As I peek over the hood of the SUV, I see muzzle flashes in one of the windows of the building next to us.

That's where they are.

"John, are you and your team alright?" I ask, turning around and looking at everyone.

"Yeah, we're good to go. We just got caught in a bad spot."

"Okay, here's the plan. I want to continue to lay down cover fire here while you and your team work around the back of the building where Dimitri's men are. It looks like they're shooting from the second floor. Can you neutralize them?"

"We're on it." John's team prepares to move, and I take up position at the front of the vehicle so I can return fire on the building.

"Ready?" I look at John.

"Let's go," he responds, starts moving from the cover.

I open fire on the window where I saw the flash of the gun barrel and James follows suit, laying down cover fire across the windows on the second floor. I take my eyes away from the building to check on John's progress. I let the breath I've been holding out as I see that they've made it to the side of the building and are relatively safe.

"James, hold your fire for a minute," I call as I start working my way back towards him from the front of the SUV. As I round the front of the vehicle, I hear gunfire from the building and know that John and his team have found Dimitri's men. I squat next to James and wait for the all-clear to ring out.

The longer it takes, the longer Mika and his team could be lying over there injured. I throw an irritated look up at the building as the gunfire stops, straining my ears to hear anything from the building.

The radio on my shoulder crackles to life with John's voice. "All clear here. We're coming out and moving to Mika's team."

"Copy, we will stay here to cover," I respond, giving James a nod. He returns before moving back into position. I move back to the hood of the SUV and watch as John's team comes out of the building, moving towards Mika's team in a quick, tactical manner.

It's radio silence for almost five minutes before John radios again. "It's all clear here; bring the SUVs to us."

"Copy, we're on the way," I respond as I run towards the SUV I abandoned earlier. James moves to get into the SUV we've been using for cover. Luckily, it starts and all the tires still have air. I follow behind James as he inches the car forward to the rubble pile where the team is.

Stopping the vehicle, I get out and meet James at the door of the front SUV, waiting to hear more from John or Mika. A scuffling sound to the right announces John's presence as he climbs up and over the rubble.

"Hey, what's the situation?" I ask as he walks up.

"Everyone's okay, they managed to get cover before the RPG hit. Mika and the rest of the team are checking some of the other buildings quickly and then will meet us here."

"Sounds good. Why didn't they answer the comms?"

"It looked like Mika's was destroyed in the explosion. I'm not sure about the other guys' comms, though. They should all be working."

"Weird…"

"Yeah, not like them at all."

I grip John's shoulder quickly and walk to James. He's leaning against the bullet-riddled door of the SUV with his arms crossed across his chest and legs crossed at the ankles.

I stop in front of him, resisting the desire to pin him to the vehicle and kiss him until his lips are swollen. Instead, I lean into his space, my lips gently caressing his ear lobe as I whisper, "When we get back to the compound, I would like to do very naughty things with you." A smile crosses my lips as I hear a quick intake of air.

I put a hand on the SUV next to his head and lean closer, pressing my body to his. The tactical gear makes it a bit awkward, but it gets my point across. I inhale deeply, taking in his scent: a mix of sweat, leather, and a purely James smell that I can't describe. Its musk mixed with a natural, woodsy smell, and it's all his.

James is breathing heavily, tickling the hair that has worked its way out of my man bun. I smile again and move back to give him space. A noise to my left makes me look at where John is standing, finding that the rest of the team is making their way over the rubble pile. I take a few steps back from James. I can't keep the smile off my face.

Mika and the other guys pile into the two SUVs we have before we return to where we stashed the other vehicles.

"While I'm glad you and James came to assist, you did disobey my orders. Once you're both healed, you will be disciplined. Got it?" Mika says, looking sideways from the passenger seat. James shifts in the backseat and glances between the two of us.

"Yes, sir. I understand." I give Mika an understanding smile and focus my attention back on the road.

We drive in silence back towards the compound.

As we draw nearer, it becomes clear that something is off. I can see a glow in the distance where there shouldn't be one.

"Do you see that?" I ask, looking at Mika and the rest of the guys in the vehicle.

"Get there quickly," Mika says. I press the pedal to the floorboard.

CHAPTER 17

James

As soon as Luke points out the orange glow on the horizon, I'm reaching for my phone to call Kee.

"Pick up, pick up, pick up…" The ringing on the other side of the phone is the loudest sound in the darkened cab.

"Kee isn't picking up. I'm trying Gray next."

The call goes straight to voicemail.

"Nothing."

"We're almost there," Mika whispers into the silence.

"Jesus, we left the most vulnerable people at the compound with minimal protection," Luke says, looking first at Mika and then at me through the rear-view mirror.

"Let's not jump to conclusions. We get there first, assess the situation, and then we make smart, tactical choices. Nothing changes," Mika responds. He seems stoic and steady, but I can see the way he's clenching and unclenching his hand. It gives away his nerves.

I glance at the two team members sitting between me in the back seat and feel the nerves radiating off them, as well.

Why didn't any of us think of this as a possibility? Maybe Dimitri was counting on us coming for him?

Did he intentionally lead us to that location and then keep us there?

I grip the back of Luke's seat to keep myself from spiraling into the worst-case scenario. I should have stayed with Kee; she's *my* partner. I should have been there with her to keep Hannah safe. I can't believe I abandoned her.

I let my affection for Luke distract me from why I'm here. I'm supposed to be with Kee, keeping Hannah out of danger, and I left at the first opportunity.

The panic hits in a wave. My chest grows tight and pain blossoms in the left of my chest as my heart beats irregularly. My grip tightens on Luke's seat as it gets harder to breathe.

"Take a deep breath, James. We don't know what's happened yet." Luke's voice cuts through the fog. I look up in the mirror to see him looking at me as he still somehow manages to navigate the winding dirt road that we're on.

I try to focus on my breathing, not the *what ifs* or *should haves*. Every breath loosens the constricting grip on my chest.

"We're almost there," Mika says, glancing my way.

I lean back and keep taking steady breaths. I can't keep the images and regret out of my head, though. All I see is Kee lying alone, surrounded by the bodies of Gray and Hannah. Or Kee and Marcus shot down outside of the house they've been staying in as they rush to get to Hannah and Gray. It's almost too much for me to handle as wave after wave of panic and nausea roll through me.

We go around a bend in the road too fast. The wheels of the SUV break loose on the gravel, causing us to fishtail for a moment before Luke regains control of the vehicle and we continue barreling down the road.

We're close now. The flames from the compound grow larger in the front window as we approach the gates or what's left of them. The gates have been blown to pieces with the remains pushed to the sides.

"We proceed with caution, no matter how quickly we want to get there. We move slowly and make sure that we're clear," Mika says as we pull the vehicles in and start getting out.

Everyone, including myself, nods our agreement. We move to get out, checking our weapons along the way. Luke immediately moves to be next to me and we all move forward as a unit, the other members of the Feather Flight Team close behind us.

The compound is destroyed. Many of the buildings have been razed to nothing but the foundations. The smoke is thick and cloying. I have to keep covering my mouth with my shoulder as we move through the remains of what these men used to call their home.

There's nothing but absolute silence marred by the crackling of the remains around us.

As we move closer to the armory, it becomes clear that the members we left behind took a stand there. There's a large amount of spent bullet casings scattered across the ground, glowing in the light of the fire. The building that was once the armory is nothing more than a cement slab and a few thicker wooden beams that are still burning.

Mika signals and we break into two teams. John and his team are going to the right while Mika's going left. Luke and I stick with Mika and his men as they make their way toward the medical center.

It's the only building that is still standing, but it shows signs of heavy gunfire. The white outer walls show signs of fire, yet the building is still standing. For whatever reason, it didn't burn like the rest of the place.

I glance over my shoulder and watch as John's team moves down the lane to where the houses are burning.

Ash drifts slowly down from above me and I feel the tugging of memories trying to pull me into the thickness of my panic. I struggle to stay present as we continue to move towards the medical building. I feel like I'm mentally swimming through tar as the flashbacks fog the edges of my vision. I draw a breath, then another, leaning into Luke as we move together.

"Alright?" he whispers.

I can't force the words out and just shake my head, trying to draw another breath. Luke takes his hand from his weapon and squeezes my arm hard—hard enough that it hurts. It makes me focus on the feeling of his grip and not on the visions swimming in and out of my mind.

"You're here, you're present, and I've got you," he says, squeezing again.

I touch his hand, letting him know that I've regained some semblance of control. We move to the right side of the door as the team fans out around it, ready to open it.

Mika reaches out and tries the handle, but the door doesn't open. He reaches out and knocks, calling out, "It's Mika and the team. If anyone's in there, you can come out!"

We all stand in silence, waiting for someone to answer the door. I figure it will either be with gunfire or a warm welcome.

Mika knocks again with a bit more force and shouts the same thing. This time, there's noise on the other side of the door. It sounds like furniture is being moved before then the door opens slowly.

We're greeted by the muzzle of an assault rifle and Gray, who opens the door wider as they realize it's us, revealing Hannah, Finn, and Dr. Hardigan behind them. Relief replaces fear on their faces as they come out of the medical center.

"Is everyone okay?" Mika asks. To our surprise, Dr. Hardigan rushes forward, hugging Mika. He doesn't seem to mind and wraps an arm around her, looking from Dr. Hardigan to Gray and Hannah.

"Yeah, we managed to barricade ourselves in here as soon as we heard the main gate go. I don't know where Kee or Marcus are or any of the other team members though," Gray says, taking a shaky breath and wrapping an arm around Hannah's shoulders.

"Alright, stick with us. We've got other buildings to clear. The rest of the team moved down toward the residential area." Mika untangles himself from Dr. Hardigan and instructs Hannah and her to stay in the middle of the group and assist Finn since they're unarmed.

I give Gray a thankful look and Hannah the once-over to make sure she's not hurt. Regret and guilt start wedging their way into my mind as I turn and start moving forward with the rest of the team with Luke at my side. There aren't many buildings left to check, as most of them are ablaze or sizzling embers. We haven't heard anything from the other team and I'm beginning to worry that Kee and Marcus may not have made it. The panic begins to swirl again.

As we move down the road, the skeletal remains of the burned houses line it. John's team meets us in the middle of the road. My heart drops as I don't see Kee or Marcus with them.

"Did you find Kee or Marcus?" I ask immediately as John approaches.

"No, there were signs of a firefight, but we didn't find any remains or signs of injury," John says, looking around the group.

"Is it possible that they escaped?" Luke asks.

"Let's move into the woods at the end of the compound and spread out, see if maybe they went that way," Mika responds.

I'm moving forward instantly and feel Luke sticking close to me as we both enter the woods at the end of the road. My heart is in my throat, the dread making my limbs feel heavier than they are. I'm suddenly exhausted and have to stop to catch my breath.

"Baby, you have to calm down. We're going to find them. I have a feeling they made it out. It's just a matter of time, okay? Kee and Marcus know how to handle themselves."

"I can't believe I left her here without any backup. What was I thinking?"

"Now isn't the time for that, James. Let's focus on finding them first." Luke rubs my back, which helps to loosen the chaos that has restricted my muscles.

I push away from the tree and lean onto him as we start walking again.

After almost thirty minutes of searching the trees, Mika gives the okay to start shouting for Marcus and Kee, as it appears that Dimitri's men are no longer around.

The woods become alive with the sounds of the team calling out for Marcus and Kee as Luke and I join in.

"Kee! Marcus!" I shout until my voice is hoarse. But still, there aren't any replies, no noises, and no Kee or Marcus.

"What if Dimitri took them?" I say, turning to Luke. "He's

done terrible things to people, there's no doubt that he'd do the same to them after what happened to Kiera."

"We can't jump to conclusions, James. Just hang in there. We'll figure this out." Luke is about to pull me in for a hug when a new yell comes up.

"We've got them!" John's voice rings out. I'm running towards it as soon as I hear what he's said. I can hear Luke behind me, keeping up as best he can in his boot.

I break through the trees and Kee stands with Marcus. I almost drop to my knees with the relief that surges through my body. They both look fine. They have some bumps and bruises, but otherwise, they are unscathed. I'm so overwhelmed that I stride forward and wrap Kee in a hug. It's the first time I've ever hugged her, and I don't want to let go. Kee hugs me back and some of the tension leaves my body.

I pull back, holding her at arm's length. "Are you okay? You're not hurt, are you?" I turn her from side to side to see if she's okay.

"I'm good, James. I'm good, I promise. Just a few scratches. We managed to get out as soon as the shit hit the fan. We couldn't get to the front of the compound, so we booked it to the woods."

I pull her in for another hug and shake Marcus' hand at the same time. "Thank you."

"Don't thank me, Kee is the one that got my busted ass out of there," Marcus says, chuckling. I keep forgetting that he's still recovering from what Kiera did to him in Russia.

"Fuck, Kee. I'm so sorry that I left you here alone. I didn't think Dimitri would pull something like this."

Kee backs up, eyeing me. "James, what is this new side to you? I'm fine, really." She pats my arm and I let go of her, stepping back and regaining some of my composure.

The rest of the team has arrived and now we can see that we're all here and safe.

"What's the next move?" Neko asks. He's got an arm around Finn, holding him up with the help of Dr. Hardigan.

"We need to find a place where we can hunker down, get our shit together, and hit Dimitri with everything we've got."

"I've got a place." I turn to look at Luke, who's just spoken up.

"You do?" I ask, surprised.

"Yeah, we can go to my house. It'll fit everyone and it's remote. No one knows about it, so it'll be safe."

Mika nods his approval, and we all move back to the vehicles before it sinks in that we're going to Luke's home.

"I'll drive," Luke says, climbing into the SUV. I climb into the passenger seat, and we pull out of the compound. Mika's voice from the back seat almost lulls me to sleep as he speaks with his contacts at the police department. They'll take care of the compound and bring out the crime scene investigators and firefighters. Maybe they can figure something out that will help us find out where Dimitri is.

I must have dozed off at some point, because the next thing I know is Luke gently shaking my shoulder and saying, "Hey, we're here." Looking around, my jaw almost drops.

The house is huge, rustic, and beautiful. It's been well-maintained from the looks of the exterior. I turn to Luke and realize we're alone in the vehicle.

"This is yours?"

"Yeah, it was my grandparents. I got my parents to give it to me."

"It looks…amazing." I don't know what else to say.

"Wait until you see the inside," Luke says smiling at me, his eyes sparkling in the dark vehicle.

"Welcome home," he says softly, leaning across the SUV's cup holders and giving me a soft, slow kiss.

I lean into his kiss and slide my hand around the back of his neck, digging my hands into his hair and pulling him closer. I could get lost in Luke's kisses, the way his lips feel on mine, the way his beard feels against mine. It's hard to complete a thought whenever he's near to me.

"Let's get inside and get cleaned up," he whispers against my lips before pulling away.

"Nnnmmmph, not yet." I pull him in again and kiss him slightly harder than before. He breathes in deeply and leans into me, into our kiss. All thought escapes me as he deepens it, his tongue playing with mine, his teeth nipping at my lip. By the time he pulls away, I'm breathless and wanting.

"Come on, or the guys are gonna think we're doing it in the car." Luke smiles roguishly at me.

I feel my face grow a little warm, but I can't keep the smile off my face. I get out of the SUV and follow Luke into his house. *His house.* As we walk through the door, I pause and take in everything around me. I thought the house we were in at the compound was all Luke, but looking around, it's clear that this is who Luke really is. I can tell where he's worked on the place, putting his own touch on the historic interior to make it his own. It's wonderfully rustic and modern at the same time. A bit like Luke.

"You like it?" he asks, standing close behind me.

"Yeah, it's great. Very you."

"Come on, let's go upstairs." Luke grabs my hand and pulls me forward and up the stairs.

Is this what it would have been like if Shawn and I had been able to buy our own home?

I shake myself to stop from going down that road and instead focus on the movement of Luke's ass in front of my face.

As we reach the top of the stairs, he steers me down the hallway to the master suite. It's got a California king-sized bed, a massive walk-in closet, and a spa-like bathroom with a large jacuzzi tub and an even bigger shower with multiple shower heads.

I don't know exactly what I expected, but this was not it. It's so wholly Luke and yet so out of left field that it's hard to comprehend.

Luke pulls me close and starts undoing the buckles and Velcro on my vest and tactical gear. He reaches down to unclip the gun from my thigh, then hooks his fingers under the edge of my shirt to pull it up and over my head. I'm trying to stay focused and in the moment, but I'm also looking around and taking in the room and bathroom.

"Do you like it?" Luke asks, gently kissing the side of my neck as he unbuttons my pants.

"It's unexpected," I reply a bit breathlessly as his hand brushes against my hardening member.

Luke pulls away from kissing my neck again to look around at his space.

"Yeah, I guess it is a bit weird, isn't it? It's a nice mix of modern and old-timey stuff, though."

"It is. I like it." I reach and cup his face, turning it back towards me and kissing him gently while starting to undress him.

My hands move of their own accord, the process of removing tactical gear ingrained in my very soul. Our kisses grow heated as I peel his shirt off and work on the button of his pants.

"Let's get in the shower," Luke huskily whispers, pulling me forward.

"I don't think I even know how this thing works. It has more shower heads than anything I've ever seen."

Chuckling, Luke turns on the overhead shower head along with one to the side. Turning to me, he proceeds to tug on my pants. I help him and am soon standing naked in front of him. Luke leans forward, kissing my chest and flicking my nipple with his tongue as he takes off his pants.

His lips find mine as he backs us into the shower. The overhead rains water down on us, cleansing away the grime from the day. Luke pulls away only to pepper my neck and chest with wet kisses as his hands run down my abdomen to grip my shaft.

I gasp, my head falling back with the overwhelming sensation of his hands and kisses. I lean back against the tiled shower wall and Luke follows me, pinning me with his body as his hard on presses into mine.

Luke grips both of our dicks in his hand, using the slickness from the water and a bit of soap to create just the right amount of friction as he jerks us both off.

"Luke…" I can barely get his name out as my head falls back against the wall. The feeling of his hand and his body against mine is overwhelming, but in the best way possible.

"That's right, baby, let go for me." Luke's lips are everywhere as he whispers sweet nothings to me as I get closer to climaxing.

"I'm close, James. I want you to cum with me." Luke's voice is strained. His grip tightens and increases in speed. His forehead leans against my chest as we both gasp for air and pray for our undoing.

My brain stops and my breath stutters as my orgasm tears through my body, my cum covering our bodies. Luke is right behind me, his climax soon following mine.

We lean into each other, completely exhausted and sated.

"We should get washed up and see what the rest of the team has figured out about Dimitri," I say softly as I draw slow circles on Luke's back.

"God, you sure know how to kill the mood," Luke kids, biting my neck playfully as he pushes back from the wall and away from me.

I immediately miss the weight of his body against mine, so I follow him under the stream of water and wrap my arms around him from behind, feeling his back and shoulder muscles tighten and relax beneath me.

"Pass me the soap," I whisper, nipping his shoulder from behind.

I lather up my hands before placing them on Luke's broad back and running them up and down, covering his back in suds. I reach around from behind and do the same to his chest and abdomen before gently gripping his shaft and stroking him with slick, sudsy hands.

"James…" Luke growls. "We cannot be in this shower any longer and this is not helping us get out of here any quicker. If you keep doing that, I'm going to fuck you in my shower."

I nip his shoulder again and stop stroking his now engorged cock. Laughing softly, I rinse my hands and get more soap, lathering myself up so that we can hurry up and get out of the shower. But for the first time in what seems like forever, I don't really care about what they're wondering. It's so…*freeing.*

I tilt my head back in the shower spray and let out a deep breath, letting the tension leave my body as I do so.

Luke's hands find mine and he pulls me close for one final, bruising kiss before he turns off the water. Stepping out, he grabs a gray towel for himself and a dark blue one for me. They're large and plush, far from what I have in my apartment.

I follow Luke from the bathroom as he walks into the large closet. A second later, he's throwing some jeans, a t-shirt, and a hoodie at me.

"They might be a bit big, but they should fit." He holds a similar outfit in his hands and starts to pull on the clothes.

"Thanks." Given how Kee and I are always in suits or tactical gear, I haven't worn anything this casual in a long time. It feels weird putting it on, like I'm shedding an old skin and putting on a new one.

"Let's get going," Luke says, motioning for me to follow him as he moves towards the door. I pause before I follow.

"Luke?" He turns, looking at me. "Thank you."

"For what?" Luke steps towards me, his hand falling from the doorknob.

"Just thank you." It's all I can say right now, even though I can feel the words bubbling up threatening to burst free.

"I'm not sure what you're thanking me for, but you're very welcome, James." Luke smiles, reaching his hand out for me to take.

Taking it, we step out into the hallway and move downstairs, finding the rest of the team resting in various places throughout the house. It almost looks like the aftermath of a frat party with people passed out on whatever piece of furniture they could find.

We find Mika in the kitchen chatting softly with Dr. Hardigan. They both glance up as we walk in.

"Are you both good?" Mika asks, looking between Luke and me as we're still holding hands. There's still a small part of me that wants to draw my hand back, but I don't. Instead, I grip Luke's hand tighter.

"Yeah, do we know what our next moves are?" Luke asks, cutting straight to the issue at hand.

"We're going to move out tonight. Garret got a lead on Dimitri using satellite images to track the vehicles they used in the attack. We think we know where he's staying."

"Which is where?" I'm getting impatient and want to end this. I'm tired of Hannah having to live a half-life. We need to take care of Dimitri so we can all start living again.

"The docks, which makes sense. Dimitri can still access his supply lines and keep an eye on everything while sending his goons out to carry out hits. There's been a lot more activity at one of the private docks in town. According to my police contacts, it looks like it's Dimitri and his men."

"How are we approaching the area?" Luke asks as some of the other team members join us, having heard mention of Dimitri.

"Why don't you guys gather the rest of the team? We might as well have a brief now so that I only have to say this once."

Nodding, Luke, I, and the other team members spread throughout the house, rousing teammates from their naps. Soon, we're all gathered around Mika, waiting for him to share information on how we're approaching Dimitri's takedown.

"Alright, so the dock is in town, but remote. The area around it is all old industrial buildings that we can use for cover as we approach the building where Dimitri and his men are hiding. We know they have a large team and access to various weapons and explosives, so we need to be prepared for anything. We're moving in as one team. It'll be all hands on deck." Mika pauses, looking around the room at us all to ensure we're all listening.

"We'll approach the building in our typical operational formation, but we'll be adding James to the formation. James, just stick with Luke and follow our signals and you'll be good."

I nod in confirmation.

"Finn, Gray, Hannah, Marcus, and Kee will be our backup, ready in the vehicles if we need to make a quick extraction. Otherwise, you all stay out of the fight. Dr. Hardigan will stay here at Luke's, and if we don't return at a certain time, she'll report it to the local authorities. It'll be in their hands after that."

Mika looks around the solemn, silent kitchen. "Do you have any questions?"

No one speaks, but there are nods all around.

"Alright. Then, we leave in an hour." Mika gets up and places his hand on Neko's shoulder. "Get them ready to go."

Neko acknowledges Mika with a slight tilt of his head and the rest of us disperse to gather our gear. We were lucky that most of our gear and weapons were saved from being destroyed in the fire after Dimitri's men attacked.

Luke takes my hand again and we head back upstairs to get our gear back on. It was nice to be without it for a bit, but now it's time to focus and get my mind right. We're going into a potentially volatile situation and there's a chance not all of us will make it out. I need to be sure that I can be there for my teammates when they need me.

I'm in Luke's room with him, putting my tactical gear back on. It smells of smoke from the conflict and sweat from our antics earlier in the day. I watch Luke dress as my hands fly confidently over my own gear, securing everything in place. He moves in the same fashion, both of us confident in what we're doing. It's ingrained in us to check and double-check our gear before moving to check each other. I feel my way around Luke's gear as he does the same for me as we face one another.

"Are you ready?" he asks, laying a hand on my shoulder.

"I think so."

"I've got your back out there. I'll be close by, always." Luke's hand moves from my shoulder to the nape of my neck. He grips it and gazes into my eyes, drilling his words home.

I return the gesture, locking eyes with Luke. He leans forward, resting his forehead against mine.

"I'll always have your back for as long as you let me."

My grip on the back of Luke's neck tightens at his words and I pull him close. "I can't think of anyone better to watch my back than you, Luke."

His muscular arms wrap around me. I return the hug.

Luke steps back after a few moments. "Let's go get this motherfucker before he does any more damage."

"Lead the way," I manage as my throat closes with emotion. I can't help but feel anxious at the moment. I'm just starting to find myself again, to find my way back to happiness, and it could all be taken from me again. I can't go through losing someone I love again.

"Luke! Luke, wait." I'm moving towards him before I can question myself. As he turns at the top of the stairs, I collide with him, grabbing either side of his face and kissing him roughly.

Luke kisses me back passionately, his arms wrapping around my waist.

I pull away, gasping for air. "Luke, thank you for everything. You've shown me that there's more to life, that I can live again, and that there's hope. Thank you for that. I need you to know that I think I'm falling for you." The words spill out of my kiss-swollen lips.

"I'm falling for you, too, James. Thank you for telling me. I know it couldn't have been easy for you to share. I want you to know that I meant what I said earlier. I've got your back, always, no matter what." Luke pulls me in and kisses me again. A lightness fills my heart.

Linking hands, we walk down the stairs and head out to join the rest of the team as they ready themselves to take on Dimitri.

CHAPTER 18

Luke

My heart feels like it's going to beat out of my chest and it's not because I'm nervous about the mission. It's because of James. Stoic, quiet, James told me that he's falling for *me* and I can't fucking believe it.

A smile tugs at the corner of my mouth as we walk up to the team hand in hand.

Mika turns to us, nodding, then continues to get his gear stowed away in the SUV. The rest of the team is getting geared up and arming themselves. James and I join in, grabbing our rifles, ammunition, and sidearms.

I'm returning to reality as my happiness buzz wears off and the magnitude of what we're about to do sets in. This is our chance to stop Dimitri from running guns and drugs in our city. Our chance to make sure that Hannah, Gray, and the rest of the team are safe. *This is it.*

Taking a deep breath, I glance at James and see that he's helping Kee with her gear. Checking and double-checking it along with her weapons. We're not making the same mistake that we did earlier by leaving them unprepared. We don't know how much Dimitri and his men know. There's a chance they are aware of my house, so we're leaving Colter, Callum, and Pete behind, all armed to the teeth and ready for whatever may come their way. Finn and Dr. Hardigan are also armed and prepared to defend themselves should anything go down.

Mika turns to look over the group. "Alright, we're clear on the plan?"

His question is met with a chorus of, "Yes, sir!"

"We stay close, move as one, and get the job done. Remember, we're going in on our own to get Dimitri, but if shit goes south, make the call to the marshals." Mika directs this to Dr. Hardigan, who acknowledges the plan with a nod and a shy smile.

"Let's go get this asshole," Mika says. The team disperses, getting in the four SUVs that line my driveway.

James gives Kee another look before following me towards the vehicle. We're with Mika and John again, and although we're both still sporting our cast and boot, respectively, Mika has agreed to let us in on the mission. We'll be in the middle of the formation, but have been instructed to stay out of the way and support the team when we engage with Dimitri's men.

I'm fine with that. I honestly want to make sure that we catch Dimitri. We have to end this, one way or another.

The car is silent for the duration of our drive; the only sound is the humming of the tires on the pavement and the occasional crackle of static from our comms as the other cars check in. James sits next to me in the back seat, quietly looking out the window, watching the landscape turn from country to cityscape as we move through the city toward the docks. My hand rests gently and easily on his thigh just above his knee, taking in his warmth before we take on the cold of Dimitri and his men.

I can't imagine what's running through James' mind right now, but he seems outwardly calm and focused. I watch his profile for any signs of distress but see none. He's a beautiful statue of strength and determination.

My own nerves start to ratchet up as we approach the docks where we suspect Dimitri has been hiding out. There's a pit in my stomach that I've not experienced before when prepping for a mission and I know it's because I'm worried about James. Every fiber wants to keep him safe and tell him to stay in the car, but I can't do that. He has just as much stake in bringing Dimitri down as I do, if not more. No matter how badly I want to, I can't ask him to sit this out. Besides, we need everyone on the team to play their part.

James' touch on my hand brings me back to reality, drawing me from my worries. I glance at his hand on top of mine before meeting his gaze. His face is fiercely set in focus and his eyes have a look I've not seen before. James is solely focused on the mission ahead and it shows by how he's carrying himself. *I'm* the one who seems to be unraveling as we zero in on Dimitri's location at the docks.

"Ready?" James asks, squeezing my hand.

"Ready," I reply, not feeling as confident as I sound.

"Alright, team. Get your heads in the game. We're pulling up," Mika's voice cuts through the comms and I imagine the guys in the other cars readying themselves for what's about to happen.

I take a deep breath, feeling the air fill my lungs before letting it out slowly, and focusing as the air leaves my lungs.

I'm ready.

Our caravan pulls in behind one of the warehouses not far from where we suspect Dimitri to be. No words are exchanged as we exit our vehicles and enter formation. We are a well-oiled machine. We move forward as one, sticking to the long shadows of the buildings.

It's not long before we hear voices coming from one of the open doors to a warehouse that looks like it should be condemned. Mika signals for John to move forward to the other side of the doorway so that we can split the entry and cover both sides on entry.

James and I move to the back of the group. We'll go in last and engage as needed so as not to slow the group down.

I take a beat, steadying myself.

Mika takes point and pushes the door open, moving silently into the warehouse with John right behind him. Each covers the opposite side of where they are entering, crossing paths with each other as they go.

The rest of the team files in, moving like ghosts and not making a sound.

The voices grow louder as we move through the building, checking the dark corners and empty rooms as we go.

We pass crate after crate of what look to be weapons and ex-plosives along with some drugs. The exterior of the building would lead you to believe that it was ready to collapse at the first strong gust of wind, but the inside tells another story. It's well insulated and maintained to keep the hardware and product safe from the elements and prying eyes.

James and I shift back to the middle of the group as we draw nearer to the sound of voices and take cover behind a large stack of wooden crates.

Mika and John move forward again as one, the rest of us fol-lowing close behind. The voices are clearer now. They're talking about moving the drugs from this warehouse to a different one outside of town. We have to stop it before that happens.

Mika signals for the team to stop and we all freeze, dropping into coverage. Holding up his hand, he motions that he sees five men, well-armed, and three vehicles.

He points to John and himself and motions that they will take the point, moving in tandem while the rest of us provide cover from the crates where we are currently crouched.

The rest of us acknowledge the plan. Mika and John look at each other, and without a word, move as one, sneakily approaching the unsuspecting men.

Time slows as they move, everything coming into hyper-focus as I wait for the gunfire to start. Mika calls out for the men to freeze and drop their weapons, giving them a chance to turn themselves over before anything else. They don't, and Dimitri's men open fire.

I watch Mika and John duck behind a few crates and fire my weapon to provide them with cover. Out of the corner of my eye, I notice James doing the same.

Bullets whizz past our heads, splinters breaking off the wooden crates as bullets get too close for comfort.

"Loading!" I call out as I duck down so that the team knows to cover until I've reloaded my weapon.

Before I can, Mika calls out to cease fire. Dimitri's men have been dealt with. I glance over the box in front of me and move forward with the rest of the team, James a constant presence at my side.

One minute, we're walking towards Mika and John, the next, utter chaos erupts. Gunfire rings through the warehouse as bullets ping off the floor around James and me. Without thinking,

I throw myself into James and we land roughly behind another low stack of crates. It does little to shelter us from the barrage of gunfire. I have no idea where it's coming from, but I know our cover isn't going to last long.

"We have to move!" I shout to James over the rat-a-tat of gunfire.

He nods and moves to get his feet under him.

We're both crouched and ready to move when Dimitri's voice blasts through the warehouse.

"I was wondering how long it would take you to find me!" His manic laughter reverberates throughout the space that has become our prison.

"Not good." James' whisper is on the verge of panic.

I reach over, find his gloved hand, and squeeze it.

"We'll get out of this," I whisper back.

I take a quick look over the box and glimpse Dimitri standing on the walkway above our heads towards the other end of the warehouse. He has the upper hand, literally. His men line the walkway, their weapons poised to take us out. Our fate hinges on a single word from Dimitri.

"I was hoping you'd bring the doctor with you as well, but I don't think it will be too difficult getting my hands on her once I've dealt with you." I can see Dimitri's psychotic smile from here. He truly is unhinged.

"We have to do something to distract him so the rest of the team can move to the stairs or withdraw for a better angle of attack," I whisper to James, trying to keep my voice steady and calm.

"I'm going to make a run for that vehicle, as I do you provide cover for the team." I point to the sedan to our left.

"What? Are you crazy? You only have one good leg—you can't

be the distraction," James whispers back while looking at me like I have two heads. "I'll break for the car and *you* provide cover." James is already moving to get his feet under him as he speaks.

"James, I can do it. I don't want you to."

"Tough shit, Luke. One of us needs to do it, and seeing as how I'm the one with two working legs, I think the debate is over."

James moves to go past me, but I grab his arm as he inches past me, pulling him down so that our faces are only inches apart.

"James…I want you to know—"

"After, Luke. Whatever you're going to say, please tell me when this is all over with. *Please.*" There's a desperate edge to his words.

James' eyes search mine and my breath hitches as my emotions gather. I think I'm in love with this man. I need him to know this. I *want* him to know.

"James, I really need to tell you—" His gloved finger presses to my lips.

"—After, Luke." Then his lips are pressing against mine. This kiss isn't like anything I've experienced before. It's slow, deep. James reaches up, placing his hand on the nape of my neck, and pulls me closer, deepening the kiss. Our mouths explore each other. By the time he pulls back, I barely have enough of my wits about me to grab the radio and tell the rest of the team what the plan is before James takes off.

I leap up and start firing at Dimitri's men as James makes a run for the sedan. Without looking away from where I'm firing, I see Mika and the rest of the team running towards me and better cover. Dimitri's men don't know where to fire and are spraying bullets left and right. As Mika reaches the closest stack of wooden boxes, John cries out as a bullet rips through his abdomen, right below where his vest ends and his stomach is exposed.

As John falls, his men behind him are already bending to drag him to safety. Gunfire from my left draws my eye and I'm relieved to see that James has made it to the sedan, providing cover for the team now as well. I let a breath out and focus on Dimitri's men again. I watch as one of my shots hits its mark and a man falls over the rail of the walkway.

I glance around and notice that Dimitri is no longer on the walkway. I don't see him anywhere. I can't let him get away again.

I glance at James, taking in his profile, then make a run for the door behind us.

"Luke!" James' shout echoes behind me as I make it to the door and burst through it into the cool night air. Pausing, I look around and see a shadowy figure running down the pier to a car parked at the end. I take off after it, hoping that the sound of my boot on the ground doesn't give me away.

As Dimitri reaches the car, I'm too far away to stop him physically, but I can give him a warning shot. I pause long enough to line up the shot and pull the trigger. I smile a little as I see sparks fly from the top of the sedan as the bullet strikes where I've sent it.

"Dimitri, don't fucking move!"

He pauses, looking from the car back to me. I move again, approaching more slowly now that he knows I'm on his tail. He moves to grab the door handle, and I let another shot go, this one pinging off the ground a few feet away.

"I said don't move!" I walk a bit faster, desperate to close the space between us.

"Show me your hands," I say, not taking my eyes off him and watching for any quick movements. Dimitri takes his hand from the door handle and turns his body towards me, both hands raised.

I'm so focused on him that I don't realize someone is behind me until it's too late. The crunch of gravel under a boot gives him away, but I'm slow to turn and Dimitri's man behind me has the drop on me.

The sound of his gun firing echoes off the abandoned buildings around us and I know I've been hit before the sound and pain register. He's caught me mid-spin and as the bullet hits, it spins my body in the opposite direction, whirling me violently around at least once before I slam into the pavement.

The air rushes out of my body as pain explodes across my chest and the side of my body as I hit the ground. I can't draw breath into my lungs. I'm seized by panic when I realize I can't seem to move my body.

Two dark shadows stand over me as I manage to roll onto my back. My vision is getting fuzzy as I struggle to breathe.

Shit, this is not how I pictured myself going out. What's going to happen to James?

Tears prick the corners of my eyes as I picture James and all the little moments we've had together in the last few weeks. I never thought I'd meet someone like him and develop feelings so quickly. I hope he doesn't hold on to this and think it's his fault.

Blackness starts to creep in as Dimitri's face comes into focus behind the barrel of his gun.

"I'm tired of this chase," Dimitri says, squatting down and holding the gun close to my chest.

"It ends tonight." He stands, leveling the gun.

CHAPTER 19

James

The distraction worked. As I crouch down to catch my breath, I look over to see Luke peering over at me. I go to smile, but it falls from my face as I see him start to turn and prepare himself to run.

Where is he going?

"Luke! Luke!" I call out after him as he takes off towards the door that we came in through, leaving me and the rest of the team behind.

I turn back to the gunfight in front of me and find that the Feather Flight Team has almost completely taken control of the situation, with most of Dimitri's men either dead or on the run. I can't leave Luke alone to take on Dimitri.

Gathering myself, I take off after Luke, leaving the team behind to finish up the rest of Dimitri's men. I'm almost to the door when a single gunshot from the other side makes my heart stop.

Not again. I can't go through this again.

I pause at the door, hand outstretched, too scared to push it open to see what's happening on the other side. What if that single shot was meant for Luke?

Steeling myself, I push open the door slowly and my worst nightmare is waiting for me on the other side.

Luke is lying on his back, clearly in pain, with Dimitri and another man standing over him.

He's still alive. He's still breathing.

We're still in this fight. I take a deep, steadying breath and aim at the man standing next to Dimitri, taking in where Dimitri is. I'll need to make two shots quickly to take both out without exposing Luke.

I kneel to steady myself, using my cast arm to brace the barrel of my rifle. I don't think a shot has ever mattered more in my life than these next two do.

Breathe in, breathe out.

I squeeze the trigger, and without pausing to see the man go down, I move my sights to Dimitri and let the next shot go. I'm up and moving even as the second shot is racing to my target. Just in case I've missed it, I want to be as close as possible for my next shot.

As I sprint towards Luke, I hear a scream of pain that registers in the back of my mind as Dimitri's. My bullet must have hit its mark. I won't stop running. Every fiber of my being is reaching for Luke. I have to get to him. I *need* to get to him, hold him, and ensure he's alright.

I come to a skidding halt next to Luke and keep my weapon trained on Dimitri. He's lying on his back, holding his shoulder where I hit him with his man lying dead next to him. I don't want to kill Dimitri; I want him to pay for what he's done. Making sure he's put away for life is what's important. I keep my weapon on him as I kick his gun away and kneel next to Luke.

"Are you okay? Luke! Are you alright?" My voice is shaking as I use my hand to feel under his vest for a wound, all while maintaining a visual on Dimitri.

"I'm okay, I'm okay. Just knocked the wind out of me." Luke catches my hand and holds it, letting his head rest on the ground. He's still trying to catch his breath as the rest of the team rushes out of the warehouse and gathers around us. Mika and Pete grab Dimitri and roughly secure his hands behind his back. He cries out in pain, but we ignore him.

Now that Dimitri is secure, I can turn my attention to Luke. I lower my weapon and gather Luke in my arms, supporting his upper body on my leg. I can feel his body shaking as the adrenaline and shock rush through him. I pull him closer as if I can make it stop.

"I'm okay, I'm alright, baby." Luke keeps whispering this over and over as I hold him close to my chest. I don't realize I'm crying until Luke reaches up and wipes my tears away while he struggles to sit up.

"Take it easy, go slow," I whisper, still holding the majority of his weight on my leg.

The rest of the team is moving around us, securing the site and getting the vehicles, yet I don't notice it until Mika is crouched in front of me, holding my shoulders.

"Let's get the two of you home," Mika says, patting my shoulder. Nodding numbly, I let Mika and the team help Luke and me up and into the waiting SUV. The vehicle with Dimitri in it breaks off from the group and heads into town, where I assume they'll be delivering him to the Marshals.

Luke leans against me in the back seat, his breathing finally leveling out. I can't take my eyes off him, off his chest.

"Let's take your vest off," I say softly, reaching for the straps over his shoulders.

Nodding, he leans forward and I undo the Velcro, releasing the vest and pulling it from his body. I can breathe a little easier now that I can see that there isn't any blood pooling under the solid black of the garment.

I run my hand over his shoulder, down his collarbone, and back across his pec. Luke doesn't move and watches me, knowing I need to do this to ensure he's okay.

He catches my hand as I go to repeat the pattern, "James, baby, I'm okay. I promise. If I were hurt, I would let you know. I'll be a little bruised, but I'm okay." I look from our hands to his stunning blue eyes.

"I was so worried. I don't think I could survive if I lost you." I lean my forehead against him, needing to feel him and be as close as possible to him.

"I'm here, I'm right here." Luke places our hands over his heart, the rhythmic beating easing my anxiety.

It isn't until I hear the car doors closing around us that I realize that we've arrived at his house. I slowly pull away, looking around at the empty vehicles.

Neither of us says anything as we sit, gazing at each other in the back seat of the SUV. I lean in, taking my hand from his to cup the nape of his neck, and pull him closer still so that I can kiss him.

The kiss is slow and sensual, full of my longing and concern for Luke. It's the only way I know how to express how much he means to me. I could kiss him forever and still not have it be enough.

Luke pulls away only enough to catch his breath, our kisses still lingering on his lips.

"We should take this inside," Luke says while gently stroking my thigh.

"Will you let Hannah look at you quickly?" I whisper into the darkness of the car.

"Yes, as long as we can continue this after she does." He leans in, kissing me passionately until I'm the one gasping for air.

"Absolutely," I manage to gasp out.

I exit the car, walk around to open Luke's door, and help him out. His limp is a bit more pronounced and I can tell that he's exhausted. Hannah is waiting for us as we enter the house, a knowing smile on her face.

"Let's have a look," she says, motioning for Luke to sit down at his kitchen table.

"Do you mind if we go upstairs to my room?" Luke asks, still holding my hand.

"Of course not. Lead the way," Hannah says.

Luke and I head up the stairs, him leaning on me for support and me taking each step as slowly as he needs me to. He's breathing heavily by the time we get to the top and I'm worried that maybe he's broken a rib or something.

We head into the master suite and memories of what we did here just hours ago flash through my mind. Luke sits on the edge of his bed and I stand between his legs to help him remove his shirt.

Hannah moves forward as I step out of the way. Luke reaches for my hand again as Hannah gently examines the bruise that is already forming over his left pectoral as I watch his face for signs of discomfort.

"You're going to have a massive internal and external bruise. But it didn't hit your ribs or sternum, so I don't think we have to worry about those. I would say take some pain medication and take it easy, but I'm not sure that you'll do either of those things." Hannah's light laughter eases the tension in the room. "He's going to be fine, James. Just take it easy on him until he's healed." Hannah smiles at me and pats Luke on the shoulder before heading out of the room and shutting the door behind her.

I return to the space between Luke's legs and lean forward into him, careful not to touch his bruising chest.

"Please don't ever run off by yourself like that again," I whisper softly, running my hands through his hair and pulling it free of its bun.

"Promise," Luke reassures me, closing his eyes and tilting his head back into my searching fingers.

I gently grip his hair, tilting his head back further, and kiss him deeply. Breathing in the very life of him, I soften the kiss. I let go of his hair and run my hand down his bare torso, feeling his aliveness.

"I need you," I whisper into his awaiting lips.

"Then have me," he whispers back, his arms wrapping around my waist before he goes to remove my gear.

I can't get it off fast enough, struggling first to remove my vest and then again with my thigh holster. I want to feel Luke's bare skin against mine. I can't get naked fast enough or keep my hands off him. I feel like a fumbling teenager as I almost fall over, taking my pants off before helping Luke with his.

"Slow down. We've got plenty of time." Luke chuckles while peppering kisses down my neck.

"I need you now," I huff excitedly back at him, finally free of my clothes. I stand in front of him again, our erections raging between us.

I can't hold back any longer. I kiss Luke, biting his bottom lip while gripping his engorged cock while my other hand grips the back of his neck, holding him close. I want to be rough, to be passionate, but I'm also worried about hurting him. I manage to rein myself in and kiss from his lips to his collarbone, then kneel in front of him, taking a nipple in my mouth between my teeth as he lets out a small gasp.

"If I'm too rough, tell me," I say, looking up at him from my position between his thighs.

"You're fine, baby. I'll let you know if I can't handle it. But please, keep doing what you're doing. It feels so good." He gently runs his hand down the side of my face, cupping my chin and kissing me before leaning back on his bed.

I continue to play with his nipples while stroking his cock, loving the way he looks as he comes undone. I run my hand down his abs and my mouth follows. I flick my wet tongue over the tip of his dick, tasting the saltiness of him before burying my face in his balls, sucking one first then the other.

"*Fuuuuck…*" Luke hisses, his grip on the edge of the bed tightening.

"Mmmm," I respond, licking my way up his dick before taking the tip in my mouth again. I swirl my tongue around the head then take him fully into my mouth and down to the back of my throat.

Luke's sharp inhale and hand on the back of my head is all the encouragement I need. I let him set the pace with his hand and the thrusting of his hips off the edge of the bed. Tonight, it's all about him. I want to make him feel good, I want him to know how much he means to me, and I want to show him how turned on he makes me.

"Jesus, James, you're going to be the death of me," Luke whispers, thrusting deep into my throat. I almost gag, but keep the rhythm going, sucking and stroking down as he thrusts up.

"Come here," he says, reaching down and pulling me to my feet. My erection is painfully hard. As I stand in front of him, Luke reaches out and takes it in his hand, then his mouth. My gasp echoes throughout the room and I can't stop myself from thrusting forward into his warm throat.

"Luke, I won't last long like this." It takes every brain cell I have to get those seven words out as I get lost in the sensation of Luke's mouth on my dick.

He leans back. "Get on the bed and lay on your back."

"Yes, sir," I say jokingly, but I can see the spark in his eyes, knowing that he must enjoy it when I call him that in the bedroom.

I crawl into bed, giving him a good view of my ass, before flopping onto my back. Luke positions himself between my legs and I wrap them around his muscular waist. He sits back and reaches into the nightstand, pulling out a bottle of lube and popping the top open.

Luke dribbles lube onto my cock and starts stroking it again. My hips thrust off the bed in time with him.

"Luke, I need you now."

"Not yet, baby. I want you to cum for me first." He strokes faster and I lose all sense of time and space, only to come back to my body when his hands are replaced by his mouth.

"Luke!" I buck one more time and climax, my cum coating Luke's throat as he swallows it down with each of my thrusts.

Sitting up, Luke smiles at me. "Good boy. *Now* I'll fuck you."

He grabs the lube, dripping it over his dick and on me, running his fingers over my entrance as I'm still coming down from my orgasm. He presses a finger to make sure that I'm ready for him.

"Relax, baby." I nod and will my body to relax around him, letting the sensations take over.

Luke presses the head of his dick against me, running it over the places where his fingers just touched. I try not to gasp as he pushes into me, but I can't help the small sound that escapes from my kiss-swollen lips.

I relax as Luke gently but firmly pushes into me. He feels so good. Every fiber of my body is focused on Luke and where our bodies connect. I can feel him pulsing as he pauses, trying to collect himself before his next thrust.

Leaning down, Luke gently kisses me, thrusting as he does so, fully seating himself into me.

"I want to go slow, but I want you so badly I'm not sure I can," he whispers, his lips and facial hair brushing my ear.

"Please, Luke, don't make me wait. I need you," I say again, hoping that he'll really hear me this time.

"James, I think I'm falling in love with you." Luke very slowly thrusts in and out as he says this, his eyes fixed on mine, our lips mere centimeters apart, our breathing one.

"Luke … I think I'm already in love with you," I whisper back, gasping as he thrusts into me, hitting my prostate and stealing my breath.

Luke sits back on his heels, thrusting deeper still as he holds my legs on his shoulders, his bruise forgotten in the heat of the moment.

Every thrust brings us closer to the edge, closer to losing ourselves to each other.

"I love you," I whisper as I come on my own stomach.

"I love you, too," Luke whispers back as his own orgasm follows shortly after.

Luke collapses onto my chest and we lay like that until the sweat on our bodies starts to cool and dry.

"We should shower, then sleep," I whisper as I run my hands through his hair again.

"I don't know if I have the energy to do that," Luke whispers back, eyes closed.

"Come on, I'll wash you." I gently shake him and guide him into the bathroom, running the shower until it's warm enough for us to get in.

Luke leans against me as I run a washcloth over his body, wiping away the events of the day and of tonight. He's almost asleep on his feet.

Once we're both washed up, I guide him back to the bed and we lay down, wrapped up in each other.

EPILOGUE

Luke

One month later

The courtroom is silent as the verdict for Dimitri's bail hearing is read.

"Denied," the judge announces.

The room erupts in applause and our entire row stands up, clapping and patting one another on our backs.

I reach out and squeeze James' hand, looking into his amber eyes. God, I love this man. In the last month, James has blossomed, thanks to therapy and trying medications that help with his anxiety and depression. He's finding his voice and becoming more open and vulnerable. It's a beautiful thing to be a part of.

Having him in my life has changed everything. I want things I've never thought of before. I know it's only a matter of time before I ask him to be my husband, to be mine, to be *with* me forever. I've never loved anyone as much as I love James. It would make me so insanely happy to have him in my life from this day forward.

"What are you thinking about?" James' voice cuts through my daydream of us both in suits getting married on the beach.

"Oh, uh, nothing, nothing at all." I feel my cheeks flush, having been caught thinking about marrying the man of my dreams.

"You okay?" he asks.

"I've never been better," I whisper back, pulling him in for a quick kiss.

"Hey, you two! Not in the courtroom!" Kee shouts from down the row. James ducks his head and I shoot her the finger before grabbing James' hand and leading him out of the courtroom, followed closely by the rest of the group.

Once we're outside, I look around and can't help but grin. We've found our people.

Gray and Hannah have moved in with each other now that Hannah's house is safe and free from all of us squatters.

Marcus and Kee are dating, and it seems to be going really well. He just met her family and hasn't stopped smiling since.

And I have James, my strong, resilient partner who loves with his whole heart.

"You are in trouble," Kee whispers to me softly as she brushes her shoulder with mine.

"What do you mean?" I whisper back, not taking my eyes off James as he talks with Hannah, his face animated and light.

"Luke, we can all see how gone you are for James."

"Who says I'm trying to hide it?" I ask, finally pulling my gaze away from James.

Whistling lowly, Kee shakes her head, growing serious. "I don't know what you've done to him, but James has grown so much in the last month. I can't thank you enough."

"I didn't do anything, Kee. James has done all the work

himself. I'm just the support. He just needed to know that he could do it, is all."

"If you say so, but for real, Luke, thank you. And if you do anything to hurt him, remember I will hunt you down." Kee pats my back, giving me a huge smile, and then walks away towards Marcus' outstretched hand.

"Everything okay?" James asks, walking up and glancing after Kee.

"James, everything is fucking perfect."

I pull him in, kissing him in front of the courthouse, surrounded by our close friends. My heart is so full it feels like it could burst.

"I love you, James."

"I love you, too, Luke."

"Good boy. Now let's go home."

Acknowledgments

I don't even know where to start. I never thought I would write and publish a book, let alone a trilogy!

I can't thank my amazing editor, Montrez, with Novel Creature Books enough. I'm not sure I could have stayed focused and motivated without your guidance and encouragement. Thank you for your feedback and the care you put into every book you come across. It shows.

A huge thank you to Hannah G. Scheffer-Wentz and English Proper Editing Services for taking on this project at the last minute and being an amazing set of extra eyes. Also, to Maddy D. for your fresh eyes and fresh takes on my work. I don't know what I would do without your final look at my manuscript!

To my friends and family, who probably think this is a silly dream but still support and encourage me, it means the world, and I don't have the words to express how thankful I am.

To you, the reader. Thank you for reading my books. This is a dream I've had since I was tiny. Books have always been my escape, and I hope that my books have been that for you as well.

Stay Connected

Instagram: www.instagram.com/ardencoutts

Facebook: www.facebook.com/authorardencoutts

YouTube: www.youtube.com/@wanderingcreativelife

TikTok: www.tiktok.com/@ardencoutts

Website: www.ardencoutts.com

Gyrating to the beat and downing shots isn't Dr. Hannah Winter's cup of tea. But when a good friend drags her out of the sanctuary of her sunroom for a rare night out at Club Midnight, a chance encounter with an enigmatic bouncer ignites an undeniable spark of passion she can't resist.

Working at Club Midnight comes with a heavy price that Gray Alexander has grown weary of paying. But even as the treacherous underworld associated with their work threatens to destroy them, the love of a sweet-faced, ginger-haired doctor may be their saving grace.

As Hannah and Gray seize their unexpected chance at love, the very place that pulled them into each other's orbit may tear them apart...

Kee and Marcus have been playing a game of emotional cat and mouse and have finally surrendered to their desires. After a passionate night together, they find themselves falling for each other. However, their newfound happiness is abruptly shattered when Marcus disappears without a word.

Confused and hurt, Kee wonders why Marcus would leave her without any explanation or information about his whereabouts. Little does she know, he has embarked on a dangerous mission.

As Marcus plunges into the treacherous world of vengeance, he faces numerous obstacles and life-threatening situations. He relies on his cunning, physical prowess, and unwavering determination to navigate the murky waters of retribution.

Meanwhile, Kee struggles with her conflicting emotions—torn between worrying for Marcus's safety and feeling betrayed by his sudden departure. She embarks on her own journey of self-discovery as she seeks answers about Marcus's motives and contemplates the nature of their relationship.

Will Marcus survive the perils he faces along his path of revenge? Will he find redemption and make it back to Kee? And can Kee find it in her heart to forgive him for leaving her in the dark?